Seduction
on the
Alpine Express

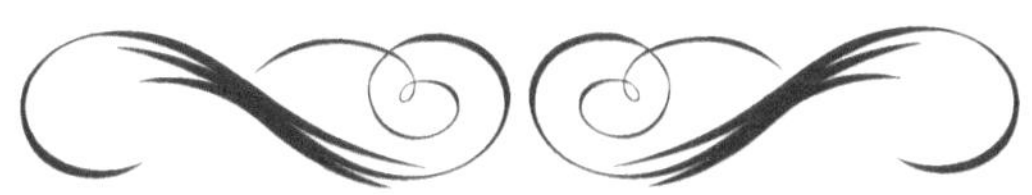

Kirsten S. Blacketer

# DEDICATION

Thanks, Star Trek Discovery for the sinful Captain Pike, without whom I would never have found inspiration for Major Montgomery.

Captain Dimples, ftw.

Also, Brianna, you sparked this story idea. I lay the blame at your feet. You're the best writer friend a girl could ask for. Thanks.

A Letter from the Author

Dear Reader,

Welcome and thank you for selecting Seduction on the Alpine Express for your reading pleasure. I truly hope you enjoy the story and fall in love with the characters.

My motto as a historical romance author has always been: If I can't be completely historically accurate, then I will at least make it historically feasible. On that note, I beg a few indulgences in the accuracy of all my stories. My love has always been for the characters first and then the setting. I use the second only to enhance the first.

I did research on the Orient Express for this story and took some liberties with the route and design of the cars. Forgive me. I tried to interfere as little as possible while still keeping it feasible.

Enjoy the adventure and the romance, let it whisk you away if only for a short time. We all need a little escape sometimes.

Sending warm regards and best wishes your way. Remember to be kind and love one another.

With best wishes and love,

Kirsten S. Blacketer

Table of Contents

Chapter One

London, England
November 14, 1888

On her tenth birthday, Matilda Hudson wanted a cake, perhaps a gift or two, but instead, she discovered her first love. Outlined by the bleak winter sky, Major Montgomery stood in the doorway of her parent's home. When he glanced down, his bewildered expression shifted to amusement at her presence. His smile revealed a pair of dimples, one on each cheek, and his storm gray eyes softened a shade.

"You must be Miss Matilda." His deep voice echoed in the hallway as he stepped inside and closed the door behind him. "It is lovely to see you again."

"Have we met?" She cocked her head to the side, her curls bouncing. He did not resemble the man her father mentioned. No, this man looked too handsome.

"On several occasions, but you were much younger. I doubt you would remember me."

She scrunched up her nose and shook her head. "No. I would remember someone as handsome as you."

His booming laugh made her grin.

"Papa is waiting for you in the study. He bade me to answer the door as Anderson is helping in the kitchen." Matilda pointed to the coatrack and danced from one foot to the other, unable to contain her excitement. "You may hang your hat and coat there."

He removed his overcoat and hat, placing them where she indicated. With his dark hair, gray-blue eyes, and broad shoulders, the major resembled her father. Yet, he seemed different. She could not figure out why.

"Come along." She snatched his hand and tugged. "I am starving. Nancy, our cook, has made me the most wonderful birthday dinner."

"That reminds me." He released her and reached into his coat to remove a small, rolled parchment tied with a pink bow. "Happy birthday, Miss Matilda." He knelt down with the gift.

"A present for me?" Matilda squealed with delight and took it. She unfurled the yellowed paper. A detailed sketch of Versailles surrounded by a maze of gardens filled the page. Her heart blossomed with joy. "It is lovely." She gasped. "I hoped to see it in person, but this is nearly as good."

"I am glad you approve." He chuckled. She swore his eyes sparkled.

Matilda hugged him. "It is perfect. Thank you." The warm scent of cloves and cinnamon and leather mixed with soap tickled her nose. Not only was he kind and handsome, but he smelled like Christmas morning.

"You are quite welcome." He gently removed himself from her embrace and stood. "Shall we see about supper then?"

"Oh, yes." Matilda took his arm. She led him into the study where her father and mother waited.

"I found him, Papa." She beamed as she clung to their guest.

"Wonderful." Her father clasped hands with the major in a firm handshake.

"Hello, Jacob." He turned to her mother who pressed a kiss to his cheek. "Diana, you look radiant as ever."

"Oh, stop, you charmer." Her mother blushed. "I see you have met Matilda."

"We are already old friends." He winked at Matilda, whose cheeks warmed.

She giggled behind her hand. They were friends. How wonderful!

"I am delighted you could join us for dinner. When does your ship leave?" Her father poured the major a drink.

"In the morning." He lifted the glass in salute.

"Can I go with you?" Matilda bounced on her toes. "Papa

said you are going to live in Paris. I long to see Paris and Versailles."

"Matilda!" Her mother's chastisement crushed her hopeful spirits.

Major Montgomery's laughter filled the room. "I do not think you would find it quite the adventure you are hoping for. This is for business, not a holiday."

Matilda pouted but nodded in understanding.

"I will visit many cities all across Europe. But I doubt I will find time to enjoy the sights and entertainment they offer." The major took a drink.

"Will you write to me and tell me all about your travels?" Matilda swished her skirts.

"Matilda Agnes Hudson. Have you taken leave of your manners?" Matilda's smile disappeared at her mother's pointed reprimand.

"It is quite all right, Diana. It would be an honor to correspond with someone who enjoys traveling as much as I do."

"I promise to treasure your letters forever." She crossed her heart. "I swear."

The major and her father chuckled at her serious declaration, while her mother shook her head. A faint smile pulled at the corners of her mother's mouth.

"Very well. I am at your service, Miss Matilda." The major dropped into a reverent bow.

A warm mixture of elation and excitement bubbled deep in her chest. Matilda's mind spun with promise of the endless tales he would tell her. She wished to explore the cities herself, but this would suffice in the meantime. At least until she was older and able to travel.

Full of adventurous daydreams, Matilda sat in the window seat as her parents and the major fell into conversation.

"I wish there was more I could do," her father said.

"You have already done too much. I cannot ask you to persist in making yourself, and your family, a target." The major paused. "I am in your debt."

"You would have done the same for me."

Matilda yawned and her stomach growled. Was supper ready? She would sit next to the major.

"You would never have put yourself in such a situation." The major laughed. "I shall miss London."

Her gaze drifted to Major Montgomery. The flash of dimples made her heart leap. Hunger and dreams of adventure aside, Matilda vowed that one day they would travel the world together.

CHAPTER TWO

Vienna, Austria
Early Summer 1896

Anson leaned against the large stone column. From this vantage point, he managed to view the full scope of the gargantuan ballroom. The portly ambassador wove his way through the crowd, his wife on his arm, and greeted fellow guests amidst the opulent surroundings. The archduke spared no expense catering to the visiting dignitaries.

The orchestra's melody floated down from the balcony. A delicate touch of longing wove around his heart at the waltz's familiar strains. He could not remember the last time he indulged in a dance. He focused on his mission. Observe, protect, and report. Nothing more.

His gaze narrowed. He scanned the room, making mental notes of those in attendance. When someone unfamiliar came into view, he pulled his notebook from inside his coat and jotted a line for each, to whom they spoke, and a brief description. Research came later.

Anson tucked his notebook back in his pocket and resumed his eagle-eyed perusal.

"Does that ever prove useful?" A deep Russian accented voice broke through his thoughts. The man's profile remained in shadows.

"Once or twice." He patted the pocket as to ensure it remained safe there.

The man slid from the shadows into the glittering light from the crystal chandeliers. "Will you put me in your little book?"

"Of course." Anson smiled. "Nikolai." He thrust his hand out and the Russian took it in greeting, his grip formidable and relentless. "What the hell are you doing here?"

"Working." Nikolai did not bother to explain further.

The years had been good to the Russian. His hair darkened, his eyes had become sharper and more aware, and his physique much broader than it was the last time Anson saw him.

His shrewd gaze raked over Nikolai. "Last we met, you were a guard at the Winter Palace. How long has it been? Seven, no eight years?"

Nikolai's expression reminded Anson of a wolf in winter, all teeth and hunger. "Nine. I now serve the whim of the Count and Countess von Breunner."

"Vash angliyskiy uluchshilsya." Anson complimented Nikolai's improved grasp of the English language.

A small smile pulled at the corners of his mouth. "My English may have improved, but your Russian is still shit."

Anson chuckled. "I see charm and tact still evade you." His attention returned to the room and the ambassador.

Nikolai shrugged. "As they have you."

A companionable silence fell between the men. They stood side by side on the elevated platform watching the nobility partake in the evening's decadence. Although they came from decidedly different backgrounds and he knew very little about Nikolai, one fateful night years before sealed their bond.

Fourteen years of faithful service to Her Majesty earned him the rank of Major as well as the honor of escorting the British envoy for diplomatic unity to the capital of Russia. In St. Petersburg, Anson played his part perfectly until it all went to hell. His reward was full culpability for an international incident.

Anson owed his life to the young Russian soldier who threw himself into the fray. They often exchanged correspondence but had not met in person since that fateful night.

"How long have you been in Vienna?" Anson stole a sidelong glance at his friend.

"Long enough."

"How long do you intend to stay?" Persuading Nikolai to speak at any length proved more work than balancing a basket of kittens on one's fingertips.

"As long as I am needed."

"You are a difficult nut to crack, surely you realize this."

"I have no wish to be cracked." Nikolai's expression remained impassive.

"How do you do that?"

"Do what?"

"Remain so serious and use humor simultaneously without effort."

"All Russians possess this ability."

Anson shook his head. "There it is again."

The ambassador spun his wife on the dancefloor. At least he made an effort in public. In the privacy of their own home, they barely spoke to one another. A flash of crimson and silver fabric drew his attention from the ambassador.

The curvaceous, dark haired beauty glided through the crowd with intent, her eyes fixed on the platform where Anson and Nikolai stood. The tiny hairs on his neck prickled as though a cold breeze drifted around him. Beside him, Nikolai tensed, his hand flexing.

As she climbed the steps, her dark eyes flickered between the two men. Her red lips curved into a salacious smile.

"*Ciao, bello,*" she purred. "Why do you stand here like toy soldiers lined up for battle?" Her hand rested delicately on her hip. A silken Italian accent wrapped around each syllable in a loving caress. "Can you not dance?"

Anson swallowed hard. The gown's beading trailed over her ample bosom and generous expanse of hip. He jerked his gaze away and cleared his throat uncomfortably.

The heat in her eyes lingered.

Nikolai remained silent.

"We are not here to dance." Anson glanced around her in an effort to dismiss her unwanted attention.

"Come now." She pressed closer, ignoring his dismissal, and snaked her arm through his. "Dance with me."

Anson shot a furtive glance at Nikolai who smirked in response. He would rub that bastard's face in the muddy banks of the Danube. The seductress pulled him down the stairs and onto the dancefloor.

The orchestra struck a lovely Viennese Waltz. Anson cringed.

"Perhaps you should find a more suited partner for this dance," he murmured.

"You make the perfect partner, Major Montgomery." She flashed her teeth in a radiant, knowing smile.

They swept into the motions, and Anson fell into the rhythm of the music and the dance itself.

"You have me at a disadvantage, *signora*." Anson glanced at the woman in his arms. "You know my name, but I have not had the pleasure of learning yours."

Her rich laughter surrounded him. "Signora Sophia Castellan."

Anson heard stories of the Italian ambassador's beautiful wife which highlighted her cunning and seductive nature. It appeared she deemed him a worthy conquest.

"*Signora*, a pleasure. But why are you not dancing with your husband?"

"He bores me." She blinked her wide, dark eyes. "I prefer a challenge."

"What makes you think I can provide you with that challenge?" His grip tightened as they spun on the dancefloor.

"The company you keep." Her gaze drifted to the platform where Nikolai stood watching.

"We are two former soldiers doing what we do best." Anson shook his head. This woman surely possessed a touch of madness.

"A soldier, yes, but also a spy." Humor and hunger sparkled in her eyes.

Anson laughed.

"Nikolai Voronia is not who you think."

"I believe I would know if he were a spy." Anson brushed off her comment.

"He is Okhrana." Her voice carried low between them. "Russian secret police."

"You are mistaken." He pulled her to a stop just as the

music came to an end and bowed. "Thank you for the dance. I must return to my duties."

She waved a hand. "As you wish. Until we meet again, *bello. Ciao.*"

Anson returned to his perch in the shadows. By the time he reached the top, Nikolai had vanished.

Disappointment settled in his chest. He searched the room, barely noting the location of the ambassador left in his charge.

"Damn it." With a sigh, he resumed his position against the stone pillar. What other secrets did Nikolai keep? Perhaps he really did not know the man as well as he thought.

CHAPTER THREE

London, England
June 25, 1898

Matilda cared little what day it was. What did it matter? Shut inside her room with the curtains drawn, she lay curled on her bed staring at the polished wooden wardrobe. Her gaze traced the inlaid design around the door's edges.

"Darling." A soft voice filtered through the door. The handle turned and a gentle light filled her room. Matilda's gaze remained fixed on the wardrobe.

Her mother sighed and sat on the bed beside her. "Matilda, you must come down and eat. It has been five days, my love. You cannot remain shut up forever."

Matilda blinked, impassive, as her mother stroked the tangled curls away from her face.

Her mother spotted the tray on her desk. "You have not even touched your food from last evening." She exhaled in defeat. "What can I do to coax you back to life, my darling?"

Emptiness filled her chest. A hollow, bitter hole that refused to be filled. She blamed herself, of course. She knew better than to believe his passionless promises. Two years, wasted on a man who never loved her. A man she never loved. The realization struck her just after she received news of his decision to break their engagement.

She anticipated heartbreak, complete with unrelenting tears and anguish. But it never came. Relief overshadowed every other emotion. The emptiness descended later when she closed herself in her room.

A void consumed her heart when she realized the man she really loved, whom she cherished since childhood, did not love her in return. But how could he know. In all the letters they shared, they only discussed their mutual love of travel. An indulgence on his part to be certain. How could a man of age and experience possibly think anything of a correspondence born of a child's whim?

"Perhaps if you tell me your thoughts, I can help." Her mother brushed her fingertips against Matilda's cheek.

She feebly shook her head.

"Well, ring for me if you change your mind. I will fetch some tea. You need your strength, my love." She crossed the room and removed the tray containing last evening's supper.

When the door closed, Matilda took a deep breath. Her mother made a valid point. She could not waste her time in such a state. Her mother's advice rang in her ear.

"'Tell me your thoughts.' Of course." Matilda rushed to her desk and drew out a piece of stationary. Her pen hovered over the page.

> *Dear Major Montgomery,*
>
> *I hope my letter finds you well. Over our years of correspondence, I've come to realize you may be the only person who truly understands me. Today, I find myself in need of a friend, someone who is not bound by the constraints of society. Your correspondence has been a comfort to me over the years. So much so, I feel I may confide in you even with my darkest secrets. However, I fear my words might alter your regard for me.*
>
> *My engagement has come to a most unpleasant end. After two years, he has cast me aside for the daughter of an earl. Yet, do not feel pity for me or fury toward his actions. I have come to realize this is exactly what I need.*
>
> *I thought I loved him. And I assumed he loved me too. His words made me believe such, and yet now as I look back on our time together, I realize his actions never reflected his admiration or consideration for me. So, this broken arrangement is truly a blessing in disguise.*
>
> *I never loved him, because I have always held someone else in high esteem. Someone who captured my affection*

*from the very moment I met him. What shall I do? I fear
he does not love me.*

I fear no one shall love me in the way I love him.

*I have dreamed of him more vividly than I have of
anyone. Handsome and charming, a prince drawn from a
fairy tale, he remains in my mind day and night. I can
think of no one but him.*

*Truthfully, I worry at my parents' reaction to the
gentleman. I have no wish to disappoint them, but it would
be wrong of me to go against my own heart.*

Would it be imprudent to confess myself to him?

*I beg of you, offer your guidance. I shall eagerly await
your reply.*

With fondness,
Matilda

After blotting, neatly folding, and addressing the letter, she sealed it. There. She set the stage. His response would surely put her heart at ease.

"Miss." Elsie's voice sounded through the door. "I have your tea."

Matilda opened the door and smiled. "Thank you, Elsie. You can set it on the desk there."

Elsie's eyes widened at the sudden shift in Matilda's mood. "You seem much revived, miss. I am relieved to see it. We were worried about you."

"I believe I have come to terms with what has happened and am ready to move forward with my life." She inhaled, savoring the aroma of the tea and sandwiches sitting on the tray.

"Oh, would you mind posting this for me, Elsie?" She handed her maid the letter for Major Montgomery.

"Of course, miss. Right away." Elsie smiled. "It is good to have you back in high spirits again."

Once Elsie left, Matilda sat at her desk and enjoyed every morsel. Her hunger returned, as did her strength and resolution.

Anticipation coiled in her chest. His response would be the confirmation she required. Then she could finally tell him of her love.

CHAPTER FOUR

Vienna, Austria
July 7, 1898

A warm summer breeze swept through the room as Anson stepped across the threshold of his small home in Vienna. Tucked in a neat row of homes barely a stone's throw from the Danube River, the location suited for both work and pleasure. Not that he ever indulged in pleasurable pursuits.

After dinner with his colleagues from the British consulate and the Austro-Hungarian delegates, Anson longed for a reprieve. After all his years with the embassy, he thrived on political intrigue and collecting intelligence. Yet, the constant vigilance weighed more heavily on him with each passing year.

His mind drifted to his friends and family who remained in England. He sacrificed his life in service to the crown but carried no remorse in his decision. Such morose longings often struck him in quiet moments, like returning to his empty home.

He placed his walking stick into the stand and his hat on the rack. With ease, Anson walked through the dark house, tugging the fabric from the knot at his throat and freeing the buttons of his waistcoat. He wandered toward his study, intent on making some notes in his journal while the evening remained fresh in his mind.

He kept a meticulous log of every event he attended, along with a list of honored guests he encountered there. A habit he began early in his career to ensure he could recall any and all information if required. One could never be too cautious.

The gentle breeze blowing through the curtains cooled the room significantly. The warm summers in Vienna sometimes made him long for the temperate reprieve of his homeland.

A flicker of movement behind the curtain brought him up short. He slipped his hand inside his jacket and rested his palm on the hilt of his pistol.

"Show yourself." Anson scanned the room.

"Going to shoot me, are you?" A breathy, familiar voice floated through the room.

Anson relaxed, dropping his hand to his side. "*Signora* Castellan." He shook his head. "You could knock like everyone else."

Her silhouette appeared behind the curtained balcony. "I could have left the consul's dinner party with you and saved myself the inconvenience."

He stiffened at her words. "*Signora*, you know as well as I do, that would not be prudent for either us."

"Would it truly be so terrible, Major?" She stepped from the shadows into the light of the gas lamp he lit moments ago. Mischief danced in her soulful, dark eyes. "I thought you enjoyed my company." A pout settled on her red lips.

What could he say? He desired her. He enjoyed conversation with her. After her husband's death, she made her pursuit of him quite obvious. The woman emanated intelligence and cunning, and it made her as attractive as it did dangerous. Every time they flirted, he tempted a fate worse than a lifetime of loneliness. A wise man would not dally with Sofia Castellan. She played for possession. Anson wanted no part of such a game.

"You are a beautiful woman, Sofia. I cannot deny it." He clenched his hands into fists to keep from reaching for her.

"Why fight it? I can see how much you want me." Sofia's sultry voice wove a spell around him. She pulled the pins from the dark coil of hair at the base of her neck. It spilled like liquid ink over her silk-clad shoulders.

"I believe you can find your way out." He stepped aside and gestured to the door. "Good evening, *Signora* Castellan."

A tense moment passed between them. Sofia arched her brow and nodded. "Good evening, Major Montgomery." She passed him, but paused in the doorway and glanced over her shoulder. "Should you change your mind..." She let the implication of her unfinished sentence linger between them before leaving.

Once the front door closed, Anson ripped the tie from around his neck and removed his tailcoat, tossing it over the back of the chair near the fireplace. Desire surged through him. His arousal pressed against his trousers, insistent. He hung his head.

Every passing encounter made it more difficult to resist her. Her status demanded propriety on his part. An affair with the widow of the late Italian ambassador would lead to nothing but ruin.

Anson collapsed in the chair behind his desk. He ran his hand over his face before reaching for the bottom drawer. A nearly-full bottle of scotch beckoned him. He withdrew it and a glass, then poured himself a healthy dram.

He hissed as it burned a path to his gut. Instantly, the apprehension faded, as did the burning need echoing through his body. He took two more drinks before the world came into focus again.

He pulled the small journal from his desk drawer and jotted down details of the evening before they faded from his mind. As he wrote, the effects of the alcohol relaxed him.

Out of the corner of his eye, he spotted the letter on the silver tray where the housekeeper always placed his mail. He cursed himself for not noticing before. He recognized the flowing script on the parchment.

Letters from Matilda always brought a smile to his face. Over the past decade, his best friend's daughter, whom he last saw on her tenth birthday, became his most steadfast correspondent. While their correspondence consisted mainly of discussions concerning travel and culture, the letters gave him a small measure of consolation. She became a beacon of light and innocence, reminding him good still existed in the world, and that knowledge kept him steadfast with hope.

He pushed his journal aside and took the letter in hand. Thoughts of his evening and Sophia flew from his mind when he opened Matilda's letter.

Anson's smile faded as he read. His heart ached with every

word.

> *Your correspondence has been a comfort to me over*
> *the years. So much so, I feel I may confide in you even*
> *with my darkest secrets. However, I fear my words might*
> *alter your regard for me.*

He knew of her broken engagement and took comfort in knowing she found peace with the situation. However, her words stung. How could anything she say alter his regard for her?

> *I never loved him, because I have always held*
> *someone else in high esteem.*

Anson found himself proud of her resiliency, but she was still young and inexperienced. Perhaps such a strong visceral reaction should be tempered. He wished he were able to better give her guidance and continued reading.

> *Handsome and charming, a prince drawn from a*
> *fairy tale, he remains in my mind day and night. I can*
> *think of no one but him.*

A twinge of envy wove between the riot of emotions coursing through him. Matilda possessed the soul of a romantic. The schoolgirl longing for a love that did not exist. How he wished he could tell her the truth, but such words would crush her spirit. He bit his lip.

> *Would it be imprudent to confess myself to him?*
> *I beg of you, offer your guidance. I shall eagerly await*
> *your reply.*

With a heavy sigh, Anson read the letter again. Guilt stirred in his conscience. For years, their letters remained full of innocuous conversation, descriptions of the cities he visited, cultures far removed from the one she lived in…but this letter held the weight of her world in it. Never before had she requested something of this magnitude from him.

He set the letter aside and poured another drink.

Guidance. He snorted. From the man least qualified to provide it. Why would she ask him, of all the people in the world, for advice on love?

Jaded and tarnished, Anson avoided such complicated attachments as indicated by his dismissal of Sofia earlier that evening. He was the last person to ask about love. The life of a bachelor suited him, especially with his complicated history and the demand of his mission.

Anson possessed a man's needs, but love never factored into it.

He sighed and tapped his fingers on the paper. Sweet, innocent Matilda. A vivacious young woman must be desperate to come to a grizzled, old relic for advice.

What would it be like to possess such a jewel? Anson could hardly imagine it. Her words never stirred such forbidden desires inside of him. Many years passed since he last saw her. The young, outspoken girl blossomed into a passionate woman searching for direction and affirmation.

Heat and shame filled him. He ran his hand through his hair and groaned. If she truly loved someone else, she should not waste time talking to him.

Anson retrieved a blank sheet of paper and took up his pen.

> *Dearest Matilda,*
> *Confession, they say, is good for the soul. Do not waste a moment longer. Tell him.*
> *I apologize for the brevity, but I believe being direct is the best course of action here.*
> *I wish you all the best.*
> *Sincerely,*
> *Major Montgomery.*

He folded the letter and addressed it before placing the seal on the back. He pushed it to the edge of his desk.

Anson poured himself another drink and paced the room, unable to sit a moment longer. Need burned inside of him. A need he could not understand. Part of him wanted to search for temporary companionship, while the other part wanted only to take himself in hand and relieve whatever perjurious desires sullied his mind.

The alcohol twisted his mind, sending decadent, forbidden thoughts into the dark recesses of his imagination. He allowed himself the fantasy knowing it would never see the dawn.

With a deep breath, Anson conjured a mental image of a fictional representation of Matilda, a woman fully grown and passionate. Her green eyes hooded and hungry. A cascade of soft, auburn curls begged for his touch. Silk clung to every curve.

He finished the scotch in his glass and sat down at his desk. Determined to purge the insanity from his mind, he put his pen to paper.

The alcohol bolstered confidence. Words poured from his mind with an ease that astonished him. He purged the feelings he did not realize lay deep within him. Emotions released by the sincere desperation in Matilda's letter.

Once he finished, he folded the letter and wrote Matilda's name on the outside. He eyed the fireplace, wishing it were alive with flame so he could burn the letter. Instead, he set it aside.

As he reached for the small tray on the opposite side of the desk, his arm collided with the half-empty bottle of scotch. The liquid spilled over the table and down the front of his trousers.

Anson shot to his feet. "Damn and blast!" He righted the bottle and ran from the room to fetch towels to clean up the mess. His head grew cloudy, and he knew he imbibed more than he should have. But the occasion warranted desperate action.

He blotted as much of the errant liquor as he could and retreated from his study. After he deposited the towels in the basket behind the kitchen door, Anson climbed the stairs to his room.

Once he removed the wet clothes, he climbed into his bed, Matilda's letter a distant thought, and fell into a welcome slumber.

CHAPTER FIVE

London, England
July 28, 1898

The servants grew weary of Matilda's persistent inquiries about the mail. A collective cheer shook the house when a letter finally arrived.

She snatched the neatly folded letter from the maid's hand. Her fingers smoothed over the familiar wax seal. Unladylike squeals of excitement echoed in the parlor. She searched for a quiet place to read Major Montgomery's long-awaited response.

She curled in the window seat and opened the letter.

> *My dearest Matilda,*
> *You must know how your words have affected me. Your letter has unleashed something inside me I cannot explain or comprehend. I dare not examine it too closely.*
> *Our correspondence has always been a beacon of light in my shadowed world. Your words bring me joy. Your sorrow brings me sorrow. When you admitted your affinity for someone, I could not help but wonder what it would be like to have someone to care for me in such a way.*
> *I hold no delusion that you could possibly love me. It is wrong of me to even covet such a shameful desire. Forgive me.*
> *Most sincerely,*
> *Anson.*

Matilda's heart swelled so full, it must surely have stopped. A weightless excitement coursed through her. She clutched the letter to her breast and closed her eyes. Warmth suffused her.

Hopeful, she read the letter again. His veiled confession sparked a desire to see him again. The last time they stood in the same room, she had been ten years old. But it did not matter. She was no longer a child. Matilda was a woman who loved him, and nothing could keep them apart. Nothing.

Matilda slid from the window seat and rushed up the staircase to her desk. She pulled a lovely piece of stationary from her drawer and penned her reply.

> *Dear Anson,*
> *I love you beyond words. I long for nothing more than to spend the rest of my life by your side as we travel the world.*
> *Name the date and time, and I will be there waiting for you.*
> *All my love,*
> *Matilda*

She pressed her lips to the paper and folded it with care. She addressed and sealed it. The passing butler groaned when she handed him the letter for the outgoing post.

Summer faded into autumn, and autumn into winter. Matilda ignored the creeping dread in her heart at the absence of Anson's reply. Perhaps he was traveling and did not receive her letter. Yes, that must be the reason for the delay. Her hopes remained high as she always received a letter from him on her birthday.

That cold November morning dawned with promise. Matilda found a letter waiting on the silver tray in the parlor.

She ripped it open and scanned the words it contained.

Happy Birthday.

Her heart plummeted to the floor. Dreams of happiness shattered at the sight of those two solitary words. Tears blurred the ink as they dropped onto the paper.

He remembered her birthday. But the stark absence of words spoke volumes. Did she say something wrong? His last letter seemed desperate and certain. Had she misunderstood?

Matilda returned to her desk and poured her heart into a reply. This time, she did not have the heart to send it. Instead, she tossed the unsent letter into the fire burning in the corner of her room. She tucked his birthday wish beside his confession of love, which showed signs of wear from repeated reading, inside her favorite book where it remained safe.

Unlike her heart.

CHAPTER SIX

Vienna, Austria
August 20, 1898

A dark mood hung over Anson. As if sensing it, the stars disappeared behind clouds and lightning flashed, punctuating the night with blinding fury. Thunder rumbled in the distance. He quickened his pace, desperate to be home and out of the coming storm.

The British Ambassador requested his company at the last several events. None of which Anson found the least bit amusing. For him, it was strictly business. All of it. The opera, dinner parties, ballets, theatrical performances, river cruise parties with dignitaries from around the world. Over the years, it lost its adventurous luster.

The briefest hint of enjoyment came from seeing Nikolai standing in the shadow of the Countess von Breunner. Their past linked them in a way most of the spoiled aristocrats would never understand.

No matter how many times they conversed, Anson could never decipher the cultivated façade Nikolai wore. Sophia's assertion of the Russian's loyalty to the Okhrana lingered in his mind. He spent the past few years watching Nikolai, but it seemed his dedication lie solely with the countess, and not the Russian secret police. He shook his head with a soft chuckle. In another life, perhaps they could have been closer friends, like Jacob and himself.

The thought of Jacob brought Anson to a halt at the steps of his townhome near the Danube. He refused to think of Jacob, because it always led to thoughts of Matilda. The sweet, trusting, naïve young woman.

Raindrops splattered against his upturned collar. He hastened up the steps and unlocked the door. Once inside and divested of his greatcoat and hat, Anson stepped into the welcome warmth of his study. He unbuttoned his cuffs as he approached the desk and sorted through the mail on the tray.

"Right horrible storm brewing outside, sir." Mrs. Jennings, the housekeeper, entered the room holding a tray with a steaming mug. "I am glad you made it home before it began to rain. Here, I brought you something to warm yourself."

"Thank you, Mrs. Jennings. I will never know how you time these things so perfectly." He chuckled.

Familiar handwriting caught his attention. He pushed thoughts of Mrs. Jennings aside as he tore open the letter.

I long for nothing more than to spend the rest of my life by your side as we travel the world.

Anson's blood ran cold in his veins. What in the devil could she possibly mean by this? Confusion racked him as he thought back to the response he sent to her last letter.

Mrs. Jennings set the mug upon his desk. "Here you are, sir."

He broke free from his confusion and turned. "Mrs. Jennings, a few weeks back, did you post a letter for me to Miss Matilda?"

"Yes, sir. I noticed you did not address it, so I took the liberty and then posted it to ensure it made the morning mail." She fidgeted at his tense posture. "Is something wrong?"

"No." He shook his head. "Not at all. Thank you, Mrs. Jennings, you may turn in for the night."

"Good night, sir."

Once the door closed behind her, he collapsed in a chair and buried his face in his hands. How could such a thing even be possible? He strained to remember the night he wrote the letter.

The evening the Italian seductress invited herself into his home. Her presence alone wreaked havoc on his restraint. He remembered telling her to leave and turning his attention to his mail, where he found a letter from Matilda.

Her heart lay tucked within each word. Until that point, he never saw her as anything other than the daughter of his best friend. The wave of fierce protectiveness unsettled him.

That explained the scotch and why he could not remember what he did with the letters he wrote. There were two, he knew that much. The first, a short, appropriate response, while the other confessed the cursed emotions coursing through his mind. He purged them in an effort to silence the damning thoughts raging against the inside of his skull.

He closed his eyes and exhaled. Of course. The spilled whisky. In his haste to clean up the mess, he forgot the letters.

Anson swore under his breath. He should have burned the incriminating letter. Now it seemed Mrs. Jennings mailed it instead.

He rose from his seat and assessed the situation rationally. He paced the length of the room, glancing at the decanter sitting near the window with obvious longing. No, he refused to put himself into a mindless stupor without addressing the issue at hand first. He did not miss the irony of the moment.

Name the date and time, and I will be there waiting for you.

Her words branded his very soul. Anson never so much as contemplated the idea of marriage. Not since he first joined the army. He preferred his life of self-imposed bachelorhood. It suited his lifestyle then, and it ensured safety for everyone now. The thought of being bound to someone for eternity, being responsible for their happiness and well-being...He shivered at the thought.

And yet, these simple words from a woman half his age brought a desire bursting to the surface, making his chest ache. His conscience cried out against the burning need. How could such inappropriate thoughts about sweet, young Matilda awaken such a beast inside him?

Anson shook his head. He made a mistake. He should never have written the letter. He should have burned it. But how could he possibly admit his error? A letter felt callous. And yet there was no other way. If he traveled to see her in person, she would misinterpret his intentions.

He threw away his good intentions and stalked over to the decanter. The burn of the liquor quelled little of the uncertainty churning in his gut.

Anson stared out into the rain-soaked night. The lightning painted the sky with brilliant flashes. The thunder echoed, rattling the glass. The weather beyond the glass reflected his mood strike for strike. His hand tightened around the glass.

The remaining solution seemed callous. Only a heartless bastard would entertain such a response to a letter filled with nothing but love and hope.

He rounded his desk and pulled open the drawer. Inside, he withdrew a box and tucked the letter inside with all of Matilda's previous letters. He replaced the box inside the drawer and closed it.

She would hate him. But he hoped in time she would realize how she misplaced her affections. She would find another, more honorable man.

Anson washed down the scream of protest choking him with the remainder of the whisky.

He sat and withdrew the journal from his pocket. He forced himself to focus on recalling every important detail of the evening. As he wrote about the evening's events into the leather-bound book, thoughts of Matilda faded.

He ignored the painful ache of his conscience bleeding deep inside his soul.

Chapter Seven

Paris, France
November 14, 1899

With utmost care, Matilda folded the worn letter and tucked it into her favorite book. She held it against her breast. The last correspondence she received came this same time the year before and contained only a birthday wish.

For months, she wondered if her confession ended their correspondence for good. She set the book aside and prepared for the special dinner her parents arranged to celebrate her twenty-first birthday.

Their trip to Paris had been a hasty, last minute change in plans. With her father serving as a liaison to the British government, he often traveled to Paris. She and her mother had not expected to be joining him on this particular trip. Yet, she did not find the short notice a burden. Not in the slightest. After all, she dreamed of Paris since childhood.

Through years of correspondence with the major, she saw many cities and countries through his eyes. But none captured her imagination like Paris. His description of the sights and sounds of the city captured her romantic imagination. His indulgence fed her whimsical fancies of grand royalty and elaborate parties which swept her away.

Every letter containing the recollections of his travels remained in a box safely tucked in her wardrobe at home in London. They remained her most cherished possessions.

Guilt crept into her conscience. She bit her lip and glanced at the book sitting on the nightstand. Dread filled the pit of her stomach at the thought of her parents discovering the contents of their last communication. Matilda shook her head and refused to ponder such a possibility.

As her father's closest friend and fellow soldier, Major Montgomery had been a part of their family for years, even in his long absence from England. However, the worn letter tucked deep in the book lying in plain view of whomever might venture into her room possessed the possibility of ruin for them both.

The letter also fostered the tiniest ray of hope deep in her soul. If only she could find a way to see him again, in person, then Matilda could plead her case. Dare she travel across Europe to confront him?

After all, she possessed several hundred pounds thanks to the spending money she saved. If she could only be certain he remained where he had been, she could act upon her plan. But such information could only be obtained from her father, who proved quite observant.

A soft knock disturbed her thoughts.

"Come in." She tempered her excitement.

Her mother entered the room wearing a striking dark purple evening gown with black satin accents. Her mother's auburn hair mirrored her own in color and style, but bore the distinguished silver threads of age. Even with the highlights, she looked not a day over thirty-five.

"Have you not yet dressed?" She tisked, bustling to the wardrobe and withdrawing an emerald velvet gown. "Your father has made reservations at *Le Grand Papillon*." She laid the gown on the bed and fussed with the hem before nodding in satisfaction. "Shall I send up Elsie to help you prepare and perhaps tame those curls?"

"Yes, please, Mama." Matilda twisted an auburn curl around her finger.

"Do try not to dawdle. The carriage will be here in thirty minutes. Your father has a surprise for you." With a parting smile, her mother left her alone.

When Elsie arrived, Matilda chatted with her about Paris. Her maid worked for the family for years. Though not quite thirty years of age, she always provided Matilda with a listening ear and sound guidance.

As Elsie put the finishing touches on her braid with pearl-tipped pins, Matilda pressed her fingers to her pearl choker and smiled at the maid in the mirror.

"Enjoy your evening, miss."

Her father's voice echoed down the hall as she approached the staircase. "Matilda!"

"Coming, Papa." She carefully descended the steps, aware of her hem dragging behind her. Breathless, she joined her parents in the front hall. After securing the wool cloak around her shoulders, she stepped out into the cool November evening. This time of year brought out her high spirits. And not only because of her birthday. She relished those final moments of fall before winter descended.

The short carriage ride to the restaurant proved uneventful. She watched out the window, taking in the sights even though darkness enveloped the city.

The marble building glistened beneath gaslight as the carriage stopped before it. Matilda tipped her head back to take in the massive structure complete with intricate gargoyles lining the rooftop and the large gilded, glittering butterfly perched on the peak of the entrance. Her parents climbed the steps, and she followed, barely containing the excitement pulsing through her.

The handsome maître d bowed and led them through the crowded restaurant.

Matilda's gaze remained focused upon their path, as a lady should behave, but she allowed small glimpses at the other patrons as they passed. Their elegant dress and manner befitted high society. She stopped abruptly behind her parents when they reached their table and focused her attention back on her family.

When she saw who awaited them at the table, her heart ceased beating.

Major Montgomery stood before her. He looked as handsome and dashing as when she met him on her doorstep when she was ten years old. Perhaps a bit more silver tinted his hair, but it lent him the most sophisticated and undeniably attractive air.

"Anson." Her father clasped their hands in a firm shake.

"So delighted you could join us."

"How could I refuse such an invitation?" He smiled, a flash of dimples forming just at the corners of his mouth. Mercy, she forgot that detail. He greeted her mother with warmth, pressing a light kiss to each of her cheeks.

When his gaze fixed on hers, the dimples reappeared. "Good evening, Miss Hudson, and happy birthday. I have not seen you since you were…"

"Ten." Matilda prayed her voice sounded stronger than she felt. Roguish and charming, his blue eyes sparkled under the light from the chandeliers. Those dimples betrayed the sincerity of his smile, and it weakened her knees.

He took her gloved hand and pressed a kiss on the back of it. Even through the fabric, the warmth of his mouth lingered.

"What a pleasant surprise." Matilda smoothed her gown and sat.

"A surprise indeed." He resumed his seat. "Look how much you have grown. You are no longer the little girl who begged me to take her to Paris."

Her parents laughed, and she forced a smile. But deep inside, she burned with pleasure he remembered her in such vivid detail.

She focused her attention on the napkin across her lap, grateful her father engaged his guest in conversation. Matilda spent much of the meal listening to her father and the major regale them with stories of their school years and their adventures in the military. Although, she noticed his careful avoidance of his departure from the military to pursue his current career.

Try as she might, she could not ignore the hum of butterflies in the pit of her stomach every time he spoke to her. Every word exchanged in every letter. Every romantic daydream. Every confession. They hung between them unspoken.

Matilda shifted in her seat. She imagined their reunion in a much different way, especially after their last postal exchange. Heat rose in her cheeks.

When dessert arrived, Matilda nearly forgot the man across

from her. Crème Brule. Her favorite. She cracked the caramelized sugar top with her spoon and lifted a dollop of the crème to her lips. Pure bliss infused her. She licked her lips in appreciation before indulging in more. She glanced at her parents who were speaking to each other. Her attention slid to the major.

His spoon rested in the crème brulee, untasted. When she met his gaze, hunger burned in their storm-colored depths. Matilda licked the spoon clean. His gaze narrowed like a hawk centering on its prey.

Aware of his focus, she smiled and finished her dessert. His countenance darkened with every bite. Matilda did her best to ignore him. Deep in the pit of her stomach, a swarm took flight, buzzing through her with awareness. She dabbed her mouth clean and set the napkin on the side of her plate.

"Will you excuse me, please?" She rose from the table, avoiding eye contact with the major.

Matilda wove through the tables once more in search of the ladies' powder room. One more moment in his presence and she would have made an utter fool of herself. Once inside the safety of the powder room, she collapsed on a settee and took several deep breaths.

How dare her body betray her in such a way? The whole meal seemed a surreal encounter. Could the major truly be looking at her with such intense hunger? The small flicker of hope sparked to life once more.

Being in the same room with him without knowing his thoughts after her last letter drove her mad with indecision. She wanted nothing more than to draw him aside and confront him. But she could never invite such scandal in public. Perhaps she should invite him to call on her at their rented home for tea the next day.

After taking a few moments to compose herself, Matilda stepped out into the hallway.

"Your parents are waiting for you outside."

She spun around. The major stood behind her. All thoughts of composure fled, especially in such close proximity. His scent teased her with those familiar hints of clove and leather. She fought against the desire to lean closer and inhale deeply, committing his aroma to memory once more.

"Allow me to escort you." He offered his arm.

Matilda nodded, unable to trust herself to form a coherent response. She rested her hand on his strong forearm. His presence overwhelmed her, and yet she felt safe beside him.

This is your opportunity. Say something.

But as they stepped out into the night, he stopped and turned to her, several feet away from the carriage where her parents waited.

"I wish to apologize for not responding to your last letter." He cleared his throat, unable to fully meet her gaze. When he did, she recognized the hunger she saw earlier, muted, but still present. "You have grown into a lovely woman, Matilda. You deserve a better man than me. *Es tut mir leid.*" He took her hand and pressed a soft kiss to the back of her knuckles. "*Auf Wiedersehn.*"

I am sorry. Goodbye. The German words echoed in her mind. Her worst fears rose like serpents coiled around her throat. Before she could reply, he pulled away and disappeared into the night.

Matilda stood on the steps and pressed her hand, the spot he kissed, to her cheek. Had she understood him correctly? Was he pushing her away, even after she saw the desire burning beneath the surface of his composed façade? She descended the steps to the carriage and pondered his words the whole trip back to their temporary home.

Her last letter floated back into her mind. Surely, he must have thought her childish and naïve for the feelings she expressed, but Matilda never felt more confident than when she wrote those words. Her mind had never been clearer. She loved him with every ounce of her being.

Could it be possible that she misinterpreted the meaning of his letter?

Matilda shook her head. "Papa." She turned to her father. "How long is Major Montgomery in Paris?"

"He leaves on the first train in the morning." Her father

thought for a moment then added. "I believe he mentioned the Alpine Express to Vienna."

His words faded into the background as a plan formed in her mind. One that would force the major's hand. If he wanted to deny the obvious, fine.

She would convince him they were perfect for each other, and what better way to do that than on a train, with nowhere to hide.

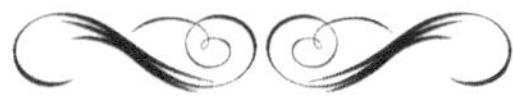

Confronting a fierce adversary would have been a more welcome challenge. At least Anson could finally put the past behind him. Miss Matilda Hudson proved to be his one weakness, and he would be relieved when a continent lay between them once more.

He stormed into his hotel room and locked the door. It was a mistake. All of it. When he realized Matilda and Diana would join them, he should not have accepted his friend's gracious invitation to dinner. But deep in the dark recesses of his selfish heart he knew it would be his only opportunity to see her again.

He pulled out the flask of whisky from his inside jacket pocket and drained the contents without a second thought. The alcohol burned, leaving a bitter taste in his mouth. He put the cap back on and tossed the empty flask onto the bed.

Anson leaned against the window frame and stared out into the night. What in the devil possessed him? He raked his hand through his hair and pulled, leaving it mussed.

He stared at his case sitting by the door. The train left at an ungodly hour in the morning. The sun would not even be up, and he would be on his way back to Vienna. This was to be a routine trip to Paris to deliver documents and ensure they made it to London. But he never expected Jacob to bring his wife and daughter.

Guilt seized him by the throat and refused to relinquish. He cursed when he remembered no whisky remained in his flask. Frustrated, he collapsed onto the bed and lay there staring blankly at the ceiling.

Young, innocent Matilda. The sweet, unassuming girl he met all those years ago with whom he exchanged innocent letters had grown into a beautiful, vivacious woman. Her rich auburn hair and vibrant green eyes were much the same as he remembered from the loquacious ten-year-old girl who answered the door. But the figure beneath the rich green velvet gown was that of a woman in full blossom, ripe for the tasting. He cursed the wicked thoughts in his mind.

Anson groaned. How could he contain the desires of a red-blooded man? He harbored needs like any other. Could he help they were polluted by thoughts of his closest friend's daughter?

"Damn it all to hell." He pushed off of the bed and tore at the buttons on his waistcoat. He slipped the jacket from his shoulders and hung it on the back of the chair near the desk. He laid the waistcoat neatly over the jacket.

As he loosened the tie and pulled it free, his mind drifted to dinner. The event went well, at least until dessert. He controlled his body's reaction, and even he maintained his composure during his conversation with her parents. But when her eyes lit with joy at the sight of that decadent dessert, his hunger shifted and intensified tenfold.

Anson lost the battle.

Matilda eating crème brulee proved more tantalizing than a woman stripping down to nothing. Innocent bliss morphed into sinful delight as he devoured her reaction. The moment their eyes met, he saw her hesitation. The way her soft lips parted in surprise. The dollop of crème on her spoon wiped clean with a flick of her tongue. The knowing smile as she finished her dessert.

It took every ounce of willpower for him to look away. To turn his mind to other things, namely the reason he came to Paris.

When Matilda excused herself, he completed his objective. Anson deposited the documents in Jacob's possession. When they prepared to leave, Anson should have departed immediately. Instead, he told them he would wait for Matilda and escort her to the carriage.

Her eyes shone with such trust, such worship, that it broke him to tell her she deserved a better man. Would the truth have been better? He scoffed.

He told her the truth in part. She deserved better than an old man with more cynicism than sense. The unspoken reality terrified him more. What would Jacob say in response to his best friend's unhealthy attraction to his darling daughter? He could not cross his friend, not after what Jacob did for him. Not after what he did to himself.

Anson sent the innocent letters with good intentions. Their relationship, a platonic exchange of sorts, focused solely on their mutual love of exploration and travel. At least it was until her confession shook his conviction.

He would not be the lecherous old man playing off an innocent, impressionable young woman. He saw such behavior in his peers, and it sickened him. No, Matilda would find someone much more suitable.

Even if he must carry his own desires to his grave.

After stripping completely, Anson climbed into bed. He fought sleep for hours, the events of the evening replaying in his mind over and over like a pathetic tragedy.

Thoughts of her plagued him until he took his traitorous body in hand and found a weak release. Doing so only made him feel disgust. How could he deny his longing? How could desire for something so beautiful make him feel so horrid?

Come the morning, he would board the Alpine Express and return to Vienna, placing Matilda firmly behind him forever.

For the benefit of everyone involved.

CHAPTER EIGHT

Paris, France
November 15, 1899

The crisp morning air stung her cheeks. Matilda pulled her wool cloak tight around her shoulders to block out the cold. She stepped out onto the train platform as the engine puffed down the track into the Paris station.

Even at such an early hour, the station seemed crowded with travelers. Matilda purchased a ticket for a private compartment on the train. The cost almost depleted her reserved funds.

She considered impersonating Major Montgomery's wife in order to force them to share a compartment. However, if he saw her before the train departed the station, he would send her back to her parents without a moment's hesitation. Instead, she developed a disguise of sorts to hide until the perfect moment presented itself.

Just after midnight, she packed a small suitcase with a change of garments, enough to get her to Vienna. She tucked her savings into the deep pocket of her gown. Matilda chose a simple black mourning gown she wore for her grandmother who passed the year before. She completed the all-black ensemble with a hat and veil, wool gloves, her sturdy wool cloak, and a lace shawl her mother had given her. A glimpse in the mirror confirmed she no longer resembled herself, but a woman in mourning.

The steam clouded the station platform as the train stopped. Matilda waited next to the building until the arriving passengers disembarked. She tugged at the veil to ensure it covered her face. If the major spotted her on the platform, her entire plan would fail. Half an hour later, they allowed the departing passengers to board. She lifted her suitcase and approached the conductor.

"*Bonjour*, Madame." He bowed and glanced at her ticket. "Welcome to the Alpine Express with service to Salzburg and Vienna, Mrs. Hudson." He waved a porter to take her bag. "Jacques will show you to your cabin, madame. *Bon voyage*."

"*Merci*." Her limited grasp of French made her grateful he addressed her in English. Her grasp of the German language lasted longer than any other language she learned in school, much to her mother's chagrin. Her entire family possessed a long lineage of French ancestry.

She followed the young porter through the train compartment. They entered the dining car and passed through the lounge car before arriving at one of three sleeper cars provided on the train. Matilda counted each compartment as they passed through the first car. There were nine compartments, three in each car. When they entered the second car, the porter stopped outside the first cabin.

"Madame, your cabin." He turned the key and opened the compartment. The scent of lemon and lavender clung to the air. "It has just been cleaned. Should you need anything, please, do not hesitate to ask. *Bon voyage*."

"*Merci*." Matilda tucked a coin into his outstretched hand and closed the compartment door. She surveyed the small cabin which would serve as her accommodation for the next several days. The shades on the window blocked the view of the platform. The train's modern electric light pulsed with a soft glow. She admired the navy blue and gold brocade seat and noticed it folded into a bed just big enough for one person comfortably. A small desk with a chair near the window served as a table. Perfection.

After stowing her suitcase in the rack above the seat, Matilda removed her cloak, gloves, and hat and placed them on the small rack beside the door. She noted the absence of a private bath and frowned. She would have to wait to use the facilities once the train disembarked.

With a sigh, Matilda sat beside the window and pushed the curtain aside enough to steal a glance at the platform. The steam swirled around the waiting passengers. Through the dim light, she spied a tall figure step from the train station onto the platform. Her breath caught as he strode toward the train.

Matilda closed the curtain the moment she recognized his face. Major Montgomery.

Her heart beat against her chest in a wild rhythm. Reality crashed down upon her. She was truly implementing her impulsive plan. There would never be a more perfect opportunity to tell him how much she cared for him.

"Patience. Have patience." She pressed her hand to her chest and took several breaths in an attempt to quell her nerves.

Matilda froze at the sound of voices in the hallway. Two distinct male voices. Had they come for her? What if her father discovered her absence and sent them to retrieve her? Perhaps it had been unwise to use her true surname. Paralyzed, she held her breath and listened to the voices. She could not make out the words, but they were just beyond her compartment door.

The voices shifted from the hallway into the cabin next to hers. She pressed her ear to the panel separating the cabins.

Major Montgomery. She would stake her life on it. Matilda leaned against the wall. For the duration of their trip, it would be the only thing separating her from the man she loved.

She pressed her hand against the wood paneling and closed her eyes.

Matilda could not be sure how long she listened for any sign of life in the cabin next door. When the train whistle blasted, she pulled away from the wall as though burned. With a glance beyond the curtain, she sighed in relief. Steam rose around the train, and it lurched into motion. After a few moments, it gained momentum, and the Paris station lay behind them.

Once the buildings dissipated and the dark sprawling French countryside came into view, Matilda stood and paced the small confines allotted her. She twisted her handkerchief in her hands before tucking it back into her pocket.

She retrieved the book inside her suitcase. In all her haste, she nearly forgot it and darted back into her darkened room to fetch it from the nightstand.

Matilda pressed the book between her hands with reverence. The pages fell open. Nothing but words printed on the bound pages. Panic gripped her. She flipped through the pages letting each leaf flutter through her fingertips as she searched. The letter was gone.

The book slipped from her fingertips and hit the ground with a solid thud. "Oh, sweet merciful heavens. No." She picked up the book again checking multiple times before tossing it onto the seat with a disparaging groan. Perhaps it fell into the suitcase.

Matilda pulled the suitcase from the rack and tossed the contents over her shoulder in a desperate search for the missing letter.

"Oh no!" Her heart dropped to the pit of her stomach. A sickening realization hit her like a gargoyle dropped from the heights of Notre Dame. "Damn and blast!" She slammed the lid on the suitcase with a deadening thunk.

"It must have fallen out." The words circling in her mind fell from her lips with the finality of a death sentence. Her parents would find her missing in the morning when they woke. They would search her bed chamber. They would find the letter. Then it would all be over. All of it.

Matilda collapsed onto the seat and stared with unfocused eyes at the wall beyond. "Papa will kill us both." She covered her face with her hands.

She jumped at the knock on her cabin door and glanced around at the mess. "Oh heavens." She scrambled to pick up her belongings and tossed them onto the seat. "One moment."

"Is everything okay in there?"

Oh, sweet heavens, the major.

"I heard something fall. Do you need assistance?" He persisted.

"I am quite well. Thank you for your concern." She winced at her poor attempt to conceal her voice. Not that he would be able to recognize her voice.

"I am coming in."

"Nooooooo!" Matilda screeched like a terrified alley cat and threw herself at the door to lock it.

The door slid open, and Matilda threw herself directly into the open arms of an extremely bewildered, concerned Major Montgomery.

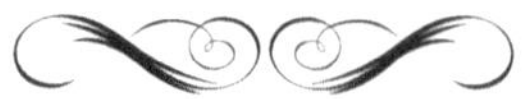

The noises from the neighboring compartment grew more alarming with every passing moment. A muted, lone voice, followed by a flutter of commotion and a series of rapid thuds. The last of which cast into doubt the safety of the occupant. He considered calling the conductor or a porter to come to his neighbor's aid but decided it would be unwise to delay.

When he knocked on the door, the woman's strangled voice surprised him. Perhaps she fell and injured herself. He twisted the handle and slid the door open. The scream reached his ears before the banshee threw herself at him.

"Are you well, madam?" He struggled to right himself and disentangle the woman who clung to his lapels refusing to meet his gaze.

"No. No, I am not." The woman slowly released him and stood, smoothing her skirt and bodice before facing him.

Rich auburn hair hung in loose tendrils framing wide green eyes he would recognize anywhere. She tucked the wayward curls into her hairnet.

"Matilda." Her name ghosted his lips in an exhale of surprise.

"Major Montgomery." Her gaze fluttered away from his and a blush touched her cheeks. "What a coincidence."

Once the shock of her presence dissipated, fury took its place. He pursed his lips.

Her mouth dropped open when he took her by the arm and escorted her into her room. He closed the door behind them. Matilda backed up, eyes wide, until she collided with the window.

His gaze shifted from her to the clothing piled atop the suitcase on the seat. He plucked the book from the floor where it lay beside a pair of black bloomers. Anson forced himself to think before he unleashed upon the woman who haunted his dreams. He glanced at the title. *Sense and Sensibility.* The irony should have made him laugh. Instead, he tossed the book on the bed and folded his arms across his chest.

"Miss Hudson, I want you to think very carefully about how you answer these next questions." He paused. "Understand that if you lie to me, I will know." He took a breath when she drew her lower lip between her teeth and nodded. "What in heaven's name are you doing on this train?"

She released her lip, swollen and pink from her teeth pressing on the tender flesh. He swallowed hard and begged his body not to react.

"I needed to talk to you after last night. Papa told me you were leaving on the Alpine Express in the morning—" she shrugged and dropped her gaze "—and I knew the only way I could get you to listen was if I waited until the train left Paris." She lifted her wide eyes to meet his, her jaw set.

Anson commended her plan. It seemed as though she considered all the possibilities. He gave her credit for that much, but her deception still infuriated him.

"Your parents will be worried about you. How will they know where you have gone?" He crossed his arms. "Did you leave them any indication of where you went? They will be worried sick."

A flash of panic touched her eyes before she glanced at the book on the bed. "Oh, I assure you. They will know exactly where I have gone."

"As soon as we reach Salzburg, I will send a wire to your father in Paris. We will return on the first available train. I am taking you home."

"I refuse to go back until you listen to me."

"I have listened to you for years. Every letter."

She arched a brow. "You never responded to my last letter."

His words died on his lips. She was correct. He avoided it and offered no reason why. But refused to do so in that moment. Not when his irritation lay so near the surface. He did not want to hurt her any further. Anson sighed. "Matilda, why are you here?"

"Because now you have to talk to me." She stepped closer. "No more letters. No more running away." Matilda tipped her chin up and faced him. Her sweet scent of rose and lilac wove into his mind threading desire through the dark recesses of his subconscious.

He braced himself when she traced his lapel with her fingertips. Anson closed his eyes in an attempt to find his bearing; his sanity. "I told you last evening, you deserve better."

"Who are you to tell me whom I deserve? I know exactly who I want. I have known since I was ten."

Anson stared at her. The words seeped into his mind. "You have no idea what you are saying. You were a child."

Matilda shook her head and another curl escaped from the net. "I have loved you for years, Major. Always you."

Her confession hit him square in the chest and tore a hole through him worse than a piece of shrapnel. "No, Matilda, you cannot possibly love me. You do not know me."

"I know you better than anyone." She cupped his cheek in her hand. The warmth of her touch sank into his soul. "The stories my father told me. The letters. The way you took the time to tell me about each city you visited. I know I was only a silly child, but you showed me the world. And it only made me love you more."

Anson's heart nearly broke at her words, but no matter how much he cared, he could not let her throw her life away on the romantic daydream of a child. He gently removed her hand from where it rested against his cheek and dropped it as though it burned him.

"I apologize for leading you to believe that there could ever be anything between us." He flinched at the look of hurt piercing her vulnerable expression. Anson pressed on, knowing his words would cut deep, but understanding she needed to hear them once and for all. "I take full responsibility for leading you astray. But I will not bind myself to a child who has no grasp of the world."

Matilda stumbled back with her hand pressed to her heart. "No, your letter, you said—"

"I said a great many things in that letter. A letter that should never have been posted. But I cannot rewrite the past." He took a breath and struck the final blow. "I do not love you, Matilda."

She straightened and dropped her hand into a fist by her side. "Is there someone else?"

"That is irrelevant. I will return you to your parents, and you will find someone more appropriate to bore with your daydreams and flights of romantic fancy." As soon as the words left his mouth, he regretted them.

Tears streamed down her cheeks. "Get out."

"Matilda." He clenched his hands into fists to keep from reaching for her.

"I said get out, you lying cur!" She snatched the book from the bed and hurled it at him.

Anson stepped to the side and it hit the door behind him. He recognized the futility of trying to mitigate the damage he caused and retreated from the room. Before he closed the door completely, he saw her collapse on the floor. Defeated, he latched the door and returned to his compartment where her sobs echoed through the wall.

The weight of what transpired hit him like a steam engine at full speed. Anson lied to the only person who loved him. To what end? Who was he really trying to protect?

Matilda.

He left his room, unable to take the guilt in silence a moment longer and headed for the lounge car where he prayed the porter would indulge his desire for a stiff drink this early in the morning. Then if he were lucky, he would drown in it and save them all some misery.

CHAPTER NINE

Tucked in a deep, plush chair in the back of the lounge car, Anson finished his second scotch. The unfortunate waiter seemed bewildered by his request considering the hour. But he tipped him so well the man poured him a tumbler of the finest liquor without question.

Regret stirred in the pit of his stomach mixing with the alcohol and making him nauseated. He stared out the window. The dawn rose over the French countryside in a vivid spray of red and orange intermixed with a deep blue.

How the hell could he have been so cruel? It was unlike him to speak to anyone in such a manner. Well, anyone who did not deserve it, especially a young woman who idolized him to the point of delusion.

Matilda loved him. He scoffed. Why? He never did anything worthy anyone's love, most of all hers. Anson hated himself for fueling her infatuation with their innocent correspondence. He would have quelled it years ago if he had known. When he received her letter informing him of her broken engagement, her request for advice gave him no indication he was the object of her affection, even though it seemed oddly specific.

Anson remembered reading it for the first time. His immediate response was less than noble. Indecision ravaged his sense. He should have sent a note encouraging her to take her concerns to her parents, not a man twice her age she met once.

As much as it pained him to admit, he bore the blame for her infatuation blossoming into something she mistook for love.

Anson did not deserve her love. He did not deserve her.

"What is this you are drinking at such an hour?" The question lingered in the air behind him wrapped in a familiar Russian accent.

"I thought you of all people would understand the need for a drink before sunrise." Anson glanced up at the uninvited guest.

Nikolai Voronia sat in the chair across from him and raised his own glass filled with clear liquid in salute.

Anson mimicked the action and finished the contents in one swallow. His stomach churned in revolt, making his mouth twist in a grimace.

"Scotch does not agree with you, my friend. Perhaps you should stick to vodka." Nikolai hid his smirk behind the glass and took a drink.

"I wish it were as simple as that." He dangled the glass from his fingertips and watched the sun rise over the fields. After a moment, he turned to the Russian. "Traveling with the countess?"

Nikolai nodded. "And her maid. She pays me well to ensure her safety when traveling through Europe. Since the incident in Moscow with her son, she has grown paranoid." He paused. "For good reason."

"Tension is growing across Europe, Nikolai. There is no stopping it." Anson ignored his guilty conscience reminding him of the past. "The countess is fortunate to have your protection."

"This is true." He shrugged. "What brought you to Paris?"

"Business with the consulate." Anson kept his reply vague, but the Russian knew more than he should. He pressed his hand to the notebook in his jacket pocket.

"Did things not go well?" Nikolai's eyes glinted in the dawn sunlight.

"Perfectly. Why do you ask?" Anson set his glass aside.

"Something troubles you, my friend. If not business, then it must be pleasure. A woman, perhaps?"

Anson exhaled the breath he did not realized he held. "Must you always be so observant, Nikolai?"

"It is my gift. Not being so would make me inept, and the countess would not entrust me with her protection." He inclined his head, and the smirk returned. "It is a woman. Who is this enchanting creature who stole your frigid heart?"

"For such a cold individual, you harbor the heart of a

romantic."

Nikolai waved the comment away. "Did you meet her in Paris?"

"It is complicated." He raked his hand through his hair.

"But you saw her while in the city, did you not?"

"Yes." Anson knew better than to blatantly lie to Nikolai. They were friends of a sort, even though he did not completely trust the Russian with delicate information. Was it wise to trust him with information concerning Matilda? Due to the limited space on the train, they were bound to see each other at some point. He sighed. Perhaps omission worked just as well. He need not know every detail.

Nikolai sat silent and waited for Anson to continue. The Russian knew how to use his presence as intimidation. A trait he admired even though it left him uncomfortable.

Anson shifted in his seat knowing even after all these years he still fell prey to the tactics Nikolai wielded without even trying.

"We dined last evening. It had been a long time since I saw her, and the event left me certain she would enjoy her life much more without my being a part of it." Anson gauged his companion's reaction.

"You left her?" Nikolai raised his brows.

Anson nodded. "She deserves better."

"I have heard that excuse before." Nikolai scoffed.

"It is the truth."

The carriage door opened with a whoosh of air. Both men turned toward the sound.

Matilda stood in the doorway. Her gaze drifted over the occupants of the car before resting on Anson. Pink blossomed across her cheeks. She snapped her attention to the path before her and strode across the lounge. When she reached the door to the dining car, she disappeared through it without a backward glance.

Nikolai turned to him and smiled with realization when he saw Anson's face. "Her?"

Frustration twisted in his chest. "Yes."

Her immediate dismissal of his presence tore at his soul,

even though he placed the knife in her hand and begged her to cut herself free. His lies served their purpose. A canyon now separated them, and it thrust him into torment.

"You do not seem surprised to see her."

"Why else would I be drinking scotch at dawn?"

"A valid point." Nikolai finished his vodka and stood. "I am in compartment eight if you need something stronger to drink." He glanced through the window into the dining car and whistled low. "But you should fix things, my friend, before someone steals her away."

When the Russian turned to leave, Anson glared at the him and swore under his breath. The blade in his heart twisted deeper. Honor, it seemed, came with a cost. Even though he could not keep her for himself, the truth remained, he was responsible for her well-being until she returned to her parents.

Anson rose from his chair and crossed to the doors connecting the two train cars. Her curls gleamed like fire even tucked into a heavy black net. She sat at a table for two, and the seat opposite lay occupied. From the angle where he stood, he could not discern the person's sex, but a fierce possessiveness overtook leave of his senses.

No, he would not interfere. She made it perfectly clear she wished for him to leave her alone. But that would not stop him from ensuring her safety. He took a deep breath and entered the dining car. The alcohol he consumed on an empty stomach made him irrational.

He sat at the opposite end of the car. When he glanced in her direction, he frowned. She conversed amiably with a woman with blonde hair and sparkling blue eyes.

Matilda noticed him and her expression hardened for a moment before she turned her attention back to her companion.

In two days, the train would arrive in Vienna. He prayed he possessed the strength to make it that long.

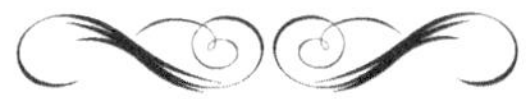

Matilda stared through the glass watching the major

converse with an unfamiliar man. Fury raged through her at his brusque dismissal of her affections. If there was another woman, he never informed her, not that he was under any obligation to do so. Never-the-less, it would have been more kind to inform her before she threw herself at him in such a way. Before he broke her heart.

The thought of his heart belonging to another woman crushed her. His letter gave her such hope. Why did he not mention anything to her father? They were the closest of friends. He would want to share his joy with his dearest companions. Physical pain would have been preferable to the ache burning through her chest and permeating her body.

Her stomach grumbled. To reach the dining car, she must pass through the lounge. Matilda squared her shoulders and took a fortifying breath. It took ages to stem the flow of tears and clean her face enough to be presentable. She tidied her cabin, checking for the letter once more while she replaced all her garments in the suitcase as well as the book she threw at the major's head.

She did not regret throwing the book and wished it had wounded him as she intended. Although if she injured him, she certainly would feel horrible. Her stomach protested again, louder this time.

Matilda steeled herself against the effect of his piercing gaze and opened the doors connecting the cars. Both the major and his companion turned. His eyes narrowed on her, and she forced herself to look away.

She caught a passing glimpse of his companion. His dark hair lay in tidy waves over jade-colored eyes. She noted the square, clean shaven jaw, and the play of a smile on his lips. She looked away, but as she passed, their gaze followed her every step.

Once she entered the dining car, she exhaled with relief. Seeing him brought the pain to the surface and threw her mind into chaos. Suppressed longing surged to the forefront. Matilda pressed her hand to her chest and closed her eyes.

After a moment, she regained her composure and searched

for a seat to enjoy the passing view while she ate. She spotted a woman sitting alone who seemed surprised to find another soul in the dining car at such an early hour.

"Would you care to join me for breakfast?" The woman's accented English made Matilda beam.

"*Sprechen Sie Deutsch?*"

"*Ja, Frau. Bitte.*" The woman gestured to the seat across the table.

"*Danke schon.*" Matilda sat. "Forgive me. I recognized your accent and became excited. I have studied the German language, but so rarely have an opportunity to use it in conversation."

"Oh, that is quite all right." The woman smiled. Her blonde hair sparkled in the morning light, and her cornflower-blue eyes beamed with warm welcome. "I do not often use my native language or English. So, this is quite a treat." She inclined her head. "I am Fräulein Gertrude Bleul."

"Ms...Mrs. Hudson. Lovely to meet you, Fräulein Bleul." She settled into her chair comfortably and folded her napkin across her lap.

"Likewise. But please, call me Gertrude. I do not stand upon formality with friends." Gertrude smiled and signaled for the waiter.

"Matilda." Matilda clung to the immediate bond of kinship forming between them.

"What would you like to eat?" Gertrude handed her a small menu.

"Oh, well." She glanced at the paper first then turned to the waiter. "Please bring me what she is having, thank you."

He nodded and retreated into the small kitchen.

"So, *liebling*, what brings you aboard the Alpine Express?" Gertrude poured tea for them both. "Sugar and milk?"

"Both, please." Matilda pondered her first question. "Honestly, I have no idea anymore."

Gertrude paused, her cup halfway to her lips. "Are you in mourning?"

Matilda sipped her tea thoughtfully. "Not exactly." She wondered how much she should reveal to her newfound friend.

It seemed imprudent to reveal everything, but pieces of the truth could not hurt, could they? Her mind ached at the conundrum.

"I do not mean to pry." Gertrude inclined her head and smiled warmly. "It is just...I know that look of forlorn uncertainty all too well."

"'Love makes fools of us all.'" Matilda sighed and set her tea aside. "I boarded this train hoping to convince the man I love that we belong together." She turned to the scenery outside as the sunlight spread over the French countryside. "But it seems I am too late."

"Has he already taken a wife?"

"Not yet. But he has implied as much." Matilda frowned. She simplified the matter, but part of her knew to keep the details to a minimum.

"*Schwein hund.*" Gertrude shook her head. "Did he lead you to believe he wished to be with you?"

"No, he did not," Matilda realized aloud as she mentally searched for any indication. "Well, once he gave me hope. But I do not think he meant to confess such things. Perhaps I misunderstood his intentions."

"Och, *liebling*, do not trouble yourself with such a man." Gertrude placed her hand over Matilda's in an encouraging gesture. "You deserve better."

Matilda could not stop her laughter. "That is exactly what he told me." She pressed her fingers to her lips.

"Maybe he is not such a *dumkopf* after all, *ja?*" Her observation lightened Matilda's heart. "But he is still a fool for leading on a girl as sweet as you."

"Have you ever been in love, Gertrude?" The connection to the woman across the table emboldened Matilda.

A sad smile spread across Gertrude's lips as her gaze drifted down to her lap. "Of course, but things are complicated."

"Might I inquire what happened?" Matilda longed for answers to her own questions through the life of another.

"Och, *liebling*, today is not for such sad tales." She smoothed her hair away from her face. "Tell me about yourself."

The carriage door opened, and the major stepped into the

dining car. Her pulse sped at the sight of him even though her heart ached. He chose a table on the opposite side of the car. Far enough as to give her space, but his gaze drifted over her as he scanned the room.

Matilda shivered with awareness.

"Are you well?"

"Yes, just a chill." Matilda returned her attention to Gertrude with a smile and turned her back on the man who plagued her thoughts.

Matilda focused on enjoying a lively conversation with her newfound companion, whom she discovered served as a maid and companion for the Countess von Breunner. She could not help but savor the fact Anson wore a scowl throughout their meal. An odd sort of satisfaction filled her at the knowledge of his discomfort.

CHAPTER TEN

No sooner had Anson settled into his seat than the other passengers on the Alpine Express found their way to the dining car in search of a hearty breakfast. He nibbled on toast and sipped the lukewarm black coffee.

Even though his attention remained on Matilda and her new companion, he maintained awareness of those who joined the train car. A handsome, middle-aged couple occupied the seats on the opposite side of the car, deeply engrossed in each other's company. A lone, bespeckled gentleman read at the next table. Two more gentlemen entered the carriage and commandeered an empty table close to Matilda.

He studied the newcomers with curiosity and uncertainty. Habit, he supposed. Years of work for the military and the embassy trained him to observe patterns and behavior. It became damned impossible for him to enjoy any time he spent in public. Even what should have been a relaxing two-day trip evolved into a mission of sorts. Keep Matilda safe. Return her to her family. Simple. Uncomplicated.

Anson finished his toast with an irritated sigh. Not bloody likely.

As adamant as he was about maintaining indifference to Matilda, he could not deny her presence drew him. Lured him, more like. Try as he might, he found it impossible to think of anything except for her.

He shouldered the blame. All of it. If he had not written those letters and encouraged her adventurous nature, none of this would have happened. Then in a moment of drunken stupidity, he made a grievous error. Even though he never intended to post the letter, it found its way to her. Bloody servants.

Matilda laughed. The sound rippled through the dining car. A few of the patrons glanced in her direction.

Her laugh drew the curious stares of the two gentlemen seated nearest her. They leaned their heads together in conversation and cast more than a glance or two in her direction as they spoke.

Deep in his chest, a shard of protectiveness pierced his heart.

All attention fell upon Nikolai when he entered the dining car. His presence alone demanded respect. He crossed the space and stopped at Matilda's table. Nikolai's focus fell on Matilda's blonde companion.

After a few moments, Matilda joined the conversation. The other woman rose from the table and followed Nikolai from the train car.

Matilda's gaze followed them. Once they disappeared from view, her haunting green eyes focused on him. He gestured to the seat across from him in invitation.

While he fully intended to keep his distance from her, Anson realized it would be impossible in such a limited space. They would see much more of each other than he could control, unless he locked himself in his compartment and refused to come out for the duration of the trip. However, his conscience would not allow him to indulge him in such childish behavior.

Whether he liked it or not, he was under an obligation to ensure her safe return to her parents. The glint of anger in her eyes revealed she too cared little for the arrangement.

He gestured to the seat once more, noting her hesitation and the flicker of indecision. She furrowed her brow and turned her back to him.

Anson shook his head. It required every ounce of patience to refrain from crossing the car, lifting her over his shoulder, and depositing her in her compartment under confinement until they arrived in Vienna. At least then he could ensure her safety without having to follow her every movement.

The gentlemen beside her engaged in a low conversation, while the couple sat oblivious to the rest of the world. The lone gentleman remained engrossed in his book.

A bundle of black fabric appeared in his peripheral vision. He looked up.

Matilda settled in the seat opposite him. "What are you doing?"

"Where else am I to get breakfast?"

"You know exactly what I mean." Her hands rested demurely in her lap. "You made it perfectly clear you desired only to be away from me."

On the contrary, he wanted much more than her company, but he refrained from indulging in that path of thought. It led only to madness. He sipped the cold coffee instead of replying.

"Of course, your twisted sense of duty and honor now extends to protecting me; is that it?" Realization lit her eyes with a fire he longed to feed.

"Your father would murder me if anything happened to you while you were in my care." He set the cup aside.

"You intend to follow me the entire trip?" She narrowed her gaze.

"Miss Hudson, allow me to remind you that it is you who intended to follow me when you stepped onto the Alpine Express this morning." He met her bold, flustered gaze. Her mouth opened and then snapped shut. "May I also remind you, this is a train, and it has very limited space. It is reasonable to assume we will be spending more time together than either of us has a desire to do at present." He beat down the unexpected delight at such a prospect and admonished himself for the thought before continuing. "Unless you would rather, I can lock you in your compartment and have the porter bring your meals."

A warm, rose-colored hue tinged her cheeks, and her eyes widened. "You would not dare." She glowered. "I am not a child. You have no guardianship over me whatsoever. I will do as I please."

Her impassioned voice drew the attention of the gentleman with the book. He peered over the top of the leather tomb and arched a brow in curiosity.

Anson cleared his throat and leaned closer to Matilda. "If

you persist in making a spectacle of yourself, then perhaps I should lock you away. A young woman, widow or not, traveling alone across Europe—" he lowered his voice even further "—is begging for worse than scandal."

"You are as conniving as my father." Matilda shook her head. "I am perfectly capable of taking care of myself. Besides, we are on a train. What horrible fate could I possibly meet aboard a train?"

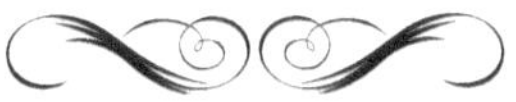

The moment the words left her lips, Matilda regretted them. Anson scowled, the marked creases between his brows deepened. He looked livid. She bit her lip. Why was it she found herself so discomforted and yet delighted by his displeasure?

"Such a flippant remark should serve as reason enough why you should not be traveling alone." He kept his voice low.

The timbre of it reverberated through her. Awareness lingered like steam from a hot bath. Major Montgomery, honorable as he was, would give her no say in the matter and escort her right back to her parent's door unharmed and unsullied. Then he would walk away forever.

Unless, she seduced him.

The wicked thought struck her with such force she gasped.

Major Montgomery's stern expression shifted to wary concern. He arched his brow but did not speak.

"Well, then." She used her sweetest tone. "If you feel so strongly about the matter, then perhaps we should come to an agreement."

His momentary hesitation made her heart pound. "What sort of agreement?"

"You wish to return me safely to my parents, correct?"

He nodded.

"I wish to see more than the inside of my compartment during this trip." She paused. "If you allow me a reasonable amount of freedom, I shall heed your advice and allow you to escort me safely back to my parents."

His scowl deepened as he contemplated her offer. After a tense length of silence, he leaned forward, his gaze penetrating into the very depths of her soul. "You will obey me, unequivocally. Do you understand?"

A coil of desire unfurled in the pit of her stomach at his tone and the demand he placed before her. "I understand."

"Very well." He looked unconvinced she would actually obey him. He folded his arms across his chest and leaned back in his chair once more. "Perhaps you should go to your compartment and rest. I shall fetch you for luncheon."

Matilda frowned. She just told him how she longed to experience more than just the inside of her quarters during the trip. But she made a promise.

Irritated, she stood. The patrons around them glanced up at her swift movement. Matilda smoothed her skirt, and with a curt nod, she left the major sitting alone in the dining car without so much as a backward glance.

A saucy retort soured on her tongue as she wove the length of the train searching for her compartment. Insufferable man. Did he not understand? Could he not see beyond his own sense of duty? She laid her heart bare, but he cared not one whit for her need for adventure and well, other things.

If he would not acknowledge the burning attraction simmering between them, then perhaps he needed a nudge closer to the fire. Being in the compartment next to his would not be enough. They needed to share one. But how could she possibly convince him to allow such a compromising arrangement?

Matilda slipped into her compartment and let her gaze wander the small quarters. Before she left for the dining car, she tidied the mess. The room sat quite undisturbed. Then a wonderful idea leapt into her mind.

"Perhaps." She snatched her luggage from the rack and tore into it with fervor, tossing the contents around the room. She ripped the case apart, pushed it to the floor, and proceeded to search the room, tearing linens from the bed and upending anything in the room not fastened down. Quite satisfied with her handiwork, she inhaled deeply and bolted from the room.

Just down the corridor, she spied Anson entering the sleeping car. She darted toward him, summoning every ounce of her acting ability. Her gasping breaths stole her speech. When he caught sight of her, he rushed forward. She collapsed in his arms, clutching his lapels.

"Matilda, are you well?" He held her close. "What has happened?"

"My quarters." She shuddered in his embrace, not from fear as she allowed him to believe. "Someone has—" she gasped "—been in my room."

He stroked his hand along her back, and she melted against him. "Stay close." He pushed her behind him and proceeded toward her cabin.

Once outside, he pushed the door open and saw the disaster she wrought upon the room. Matilda attempted to maintain the mixture of shock and fear on her expression as he searched her quarters.

He turned to her. "What on earth were they searching for?"

Matilda shook her head and bit her lip. She did not think that far ahead in her plan and kicked herself.

Anson lifted the suitcase onto the bed.

She paused beside him, searching his face. His expression darkened as he drifted deeper in thought.

"Is something wrong?" Concern bloomed through her.

"Wait here." He left, and she heard him swear through the open door.

Matilda darted into the corridor. Anson stood in the doorway of his own compartment. He ran his hand across his jaw roughly before swearing again.

"What is it?" She edged toward him.

Matilda peered around his broad figure. Inside, the same chaos from her own quarters mirrored in his. Anson's luggage lay ripped apart. His clothes and documents strewn around the room. The bed tossed in shambles, shredded linen everywhere. Even his suitcase lining gaped in jagged tatters.

With a gasp, Matilda drew back with genuine shock. Her heart hammered in her chest. She placed her other hand over it to stop the pounding. How could this be possible? She only meant to force Anson's hand and make her stay with him. But this, this was beyond anything she ever expected. Her gaze rested on the man beside her as he scoured the room.

Who could have done this? In that moment, she longed to tell Anson the truth. To confess her plan and explain her room had not been searched as his had. Shame washed over her, and the words curdled in her mouth.

Anson turned. "Matilda, go into your compartment, close the door, and lock it."

Matilda nodded, but the action felt distant, detached as though she retained no control over her body.

"Go, now."

She returned to her compartment and paused in the doorway. "Where are you going?"

"To find the porter and the conductor." He nudged her into her room. "Close this door and lock it. I do not want you to open it for anyone except me. Do you understand?"

Tears welled in her eyes. Matilda nodded, and he left her. She slid the bolt closed and leaned against the door. Panic filled her. Guilt gripped her. How could she have contemplated such a ruse when the reality caused her this much panic?

Flushed with shame and disappointment in herself, she sat on the edge of the bed and stared at the mess. How could she possibly tell him the truth? While it was the proper course of action, Matilda could not bring herself to even imagine the disappointment and anger Anson would feel at her careless actions.

Alone with burning regret, Matilda righted her room once more, ignoring the painful ache in her chest reminding her how foolhardy she behaved. She should have stayed in Paris.

Chapter Eleven

Anson relaxed at the click of the lock sliding into place. He waited to ensure she would remain in her room as he requested. After a few minutes, he closed the door to his own compartment before heading down the corridor.

Two thoughts occupied his mind. Who ransacked his quarters? If they were looking for the packet of documents from the embassy, they were too late. That was the only thing of importance he carried. What were they hoping to find?

The porter stood at the entrance to the next carriage.

"Pardon me."

The porter turned. "May I help you, sir?"

"Yes, I wish to report an incident." Anson chose not to mention Matilda.

The porter's eyes widened in alarm. "I will summon the conductor at once."

Anson nodded. "Compartment number five."

"At once, sir." The porter bowed and hurtled down the corridor with barely contained decorum.

He sighed and returned to the car containing his own quarters. He would verify the state of the room with the train employees, but for the moment, the rest of the passengers need not be concerned with the incident. Not that he wished to keep them from panic. No, the truth was far less honorable. Whoever ransacked his compartment was on this train, and he intended to find them out.

Anson would discover the culprit before they reached their first stop in Salzburg, even if he needed to interrogate every passenger and employee.

He paused outside his room. His gaze strayed to the next compartment. The memory of Matilda rushing down the corridor launching herself into his arms surfaced in his mind. In that moment, he believed her. When he saw her room in disarray, uncertainty gnawed at his insides. He found his need to protect Matilda tripled once he saw his own room sacked in a similar manner.

Then he allowed his emotions to subside long enough to compare the carnage of the two rooms.

Anson shook his head. How foolish could he be? If she believed him to be both blind and stupid, then she was in for a startling revelation. Objectively comparing the two led him to only one conclusion. She tossed her own room. But why?

He ignored the urge to beat down her door, turn her over his knee, and demand answers. Instead, he entered his room and once again surveyed the damage. He would deal with her later.

Several moments later, the porter accompanied by the conductor appeared the doorway. He noted their shocked expressions.

"As you can see, someone has sacked my compartment." Anson gestured to the disaster.

"Have you any idea who may have done this, sir?" The portly conductor wiped his brow.

"No. But I would appreciate if you would keep this matter between us for the moment. I do not wish to alarm the other passengers." He offered a card showing his credentials as a liaison to the British embassy.

"Of course." The conductor's gaze skimmed over the room several times. He cleared his throat and smoothed his thin mustache before speaking. "Was anything taken?"

"Not that I can see." Anson lifted his suitcase and set it on the bed. "But I intend to do a full inventory."

"Very well, sir. If there is anything you require, please do not hesitate to notify us." The conductor gestured to the porter Anson spoke with earlier.

"Thank you. I will require new bedding. Two sets, if you please."

The porter nodded and disappeared down the corridor.

"We will be arriving in Salzburg tomorrow evening. Would

you like me to send a telegram alerting the authorities in Paris about this incident?" The conductor kept his voice low in case any other passengers happened to pass by.

"No, thank you. I will report it myself." Anson stepped closer. "It may be prudent to watch for any suspicious activity."

"Agreed." The conductor straightened his waistcoat and checked his watch. "If you will excuse me, I must attend to my schedule."

Anson nodded, and the conductor retreated.

As he gathered his belongings off the floor and laid them on the bed, he shuffled through his first impressions of each passenger in the dining car that morning. He rotated through them by table.

The two gentlemen. The mature couple. The lone, bespeckled gentleman. Matilda and her new acquaintance. There were only two passengers not accounted for on the train in the dining car during that time. The countess and her bodyguard, Nikolai.

Anson's gaze narrowed at the scattered clothing on the bed. The countess would not stoop low enough to ransack his room. What purpose would it serve? No, if she desired something he possessed, she would have sent someone to do the dirty work. Someone at her behest. *Nikolai.*

They were professional acquaintances and harbored a tenuous friendship at best. But there was always a mutual respect and understanding between them since that horrid night in St. Petersburg.

Unless his room was targeted while Nikolai sat with him in the lounge. Still, it made no sense. Whoever searched his room wanted something. But Anson knew beyond a doubt there was nothing for them to find. He delivered the confidential intelligence in Paris. Jacob assured him it would reach London post haste.

What in the devil could they have been searching for?

With a sigh, Anson shook his head and replaced his clothing in the suitcase.

The porter returned bearing two sets of linens. He set them

on the bed and gathered the ruined linens from the floor. After the man retreated, Anson stared at the pile, deep in thought.

He gathered one set in his arms and stepped out into the hallway. Apprehension twisted in his gut as he stood before Matilda's door. He pushed it away and knocked.

"Who is it?"

"Major Montgomery."

The bolt clicked, and the door opened. Matilda confirmed his identity through a crack in the door before opening it and stepping aside to allow him entrance. Once he entered, she closed the door behind him.

Her suitcase lay in the rack above the seat. The linens replaced neatly. Even her wayward curls were tamed, pinned under the black net.

She twisted her hands together. "Did they take anything?"

"No."

"Good." She nibbled her lower lip and dropped her gaze.

He placed the linens on the bed and folded his arms across his chest. "Matilda."

Her green gaze snapped up. His heart hammered at the innocent hunger in their depths. The confidence he expected from her melted under his scrutiny. Her attention fluttered away from his bold gaze.

"Is something bothering you?" He followed the suspicion burning in his gut. The outspoken young woman he knew lurked beneath the proper exterior suddenly withdrew. "If you wish to leave this compartment before we reach Vienna, you will tell me the truth."

Her attention refocused on him. The impassioned blaze of defiance ignited once more. Her lips thinned as she pressed them together. Her brow furrowed deepening her scowl.

They faced each other locked in a silent battle of wills. Anson remained impassive, unmovable like an ancient oak.

She sighed in defeat. "Fine. I did it."

"You tore my room apart?" He baited her. The truth lingered in the back of his mind the moment he saw her reaction to his compartment. Shock and horror. Much more believable than the show she presented when she found her own room turned upside down.

"No!" Her eyes widened, and she shook her head. "No. I would never—" She heaved a heavy sigh and paced the small space. "My room. I tossed my room." She faced him once more, fury and embarrassment leaving a scarlet stain across her cheeks.

Victory. Anson refrained from indulging in a satisfied smirk. Instead, he frowned and shook his head, feigning disappointment. She wished to behave like a child. Then he would treat her like one.

"Why?"

She picked at a frayed hem on her gown sleeve.

"I can easily post guard outside your door for the remainder of the trip, if that is what you choose." Anson would pull the truth from her if it took him the entire day.

"Do you enjoy in treating me like I am an unruly child?" She glared at him.

"If you want to be treated like an adult, Matilda, then you must behave like one."

She threw her hands up. "Fine. But promise you will not lock me in this room first."

"I promise if you tell me the truth, then I will allow you some freedom." He saw the indecision flicker across her features. He enjoyed watching the play of emotions on her beautiful face.

He shook the dangerous thoughts from his mind. He would not indulge in whatever flirtatious ideas teased their way into his imagination.

"I wanted you to believe I was in danger and force me to stay in your compartment." Her voice trailed off on the last part of the sentence.

But he heard every word. A bolt of need shot through him. He wanted it more than he ever dare admit, even to himself. The need to keep her as close to him as possible terrified him.

When he did not respond, she continued. "I wanted to spend as much time with you as I could before you take me back to my parents. Before you leave and forget all about me."

Dumbstruck, he stood staring at her profile. The softest blush stole across her cheeks and down her throat when she turned to face him.

Anson wanted to shake her and kiss her in equal parts. He ran a hand through his hair. "Goddamn it, Matilda."

Before he released the beast struggling inside, he turned and left the compartment. He got the answers he searched for all right, but they did not satisfy him. Nothing would.

Nothing except Matilda in his arms and in his bed. And that would never happen.

CHAPTER TWELVE

No one could ever accuse Matilda Hudson of being selfish. In fact, over the past several years she volunteered much of her time to helping the nuns at St. Agnes' Orphanage in an odd assortment of ways. And yet, she sat in the train compartment alone and disappointed with the current turn of events feeling sorry for herself.

Matilda scowled at the wall shared with the man who drove her to the brink of madness.

Honestly, she longed for nothing more than to chuck a solid brick at his head. Multiple, if possible. Twice in the past twelve hours, she made an utter fool of herself. And twice he shunned her.

Matilda crossed her arms and harrumphed. Not that it mattered one whit. Major Montgomery left her hanging like a bit of linen forgotten outside in the rain. If he rejected her, then she could respect his decision and move on with her life. In the meantime, she yearned for whatever company he offered before he disappeared forever.

Perhaps she crossed the line by attempting to trick him. She groaned. Did she really believe herself capable of fooling him? Or seducing him? Honestly, what came over her?

Desperation. Pure, unfettered desperation. It lingered still in the darkest recesses of her soul.

"Foolish idiot. How could you possibly imagine he would fall for your pathetic scheme?"

Perhaps the answer lay upon another path. If he was not moved by her words, then perhaps her actions might ignite something between them.

Matilda realized she held no true understanding of what seduction entailed. She drew knowledge from novels and observations at social gatherings, but these, she knew, were more flirtations than seduction.

A knock stirred the sullen silence around her.

She opened the latch, not bothering to ask who intruded upon her solitude.

The major stood before her with a deep crease between his brows and a frown marring his full lips. No dimpled smile greeted her. A pang of frustration shot through her heart. She longed to see that fleeting smile she glimpsed at dinner the evening before.

"I have come to escort you to the dining car for luncheon." He gestured for her to lead the way.

Matilda swept past him. "Must you make it sound so much like a detested chore?" She cast him a look over her shoulder.

He did not respond.

She squared her shoulders and approached the door to the lounge car where they encountered the bespeckled gentleman from earlier.

"Good afternoon." The gentleman smiled. He nodded to both her and the major.

"Good afternoon." Matilda grinned, delighted with the chance to mingle with the other passengers.

"Doctor Phineas Archer, at your service, madam." His brown eyes sparkled behind his glasses. A French accent wrapped around every syllable.

"Mrs. Hudson, and this is my traveling companion, Mr. Montgomery. Very delighted to make your acquaintance, sir."

Dr. Archer's curious gaze flickered between them. A smile curled beneath his bushy mustache. "A pleasure indeed, madam. If you will pardon me, I must find the porter. It seems I have misplaced my book."

"Oh, well I hope you find it." Matilda stepped aside for him to pass.

"*Merci.*" He inclined his head to both of them.

Matilda watched him shuffle down the hallway. When she caught sight of the major's irritated expression, she turned away with a swish of her skirts and entered the lounge to cross into the dining car.

The two gentlemen from breakfast sat in the lounge near the window, their heads bowed together in conversation. Curiosity pricked at her. The dark-haired one glanced up and their eyes met for a moment. She turned her attention away, and a shiver of unease coursed through her.

They entered the dining car where Matilda breathed a sigh of relief. Gertrude sat at the same table they shared earlier that morning. She glanced up as Matilda entered the dining car and smiled.

The gentleman whom she met earlier, Mr. Voronia, sat with Gertrude. His dark head turned, his intense gaze following her.

Mr. Voronia's lip curled into a small courteous smile as he rose from his seat. "Please, sit down, Mrs. Hudson. My companion is quite tired of my company." His deep voice mixed with the thick Russian accent made her shiver. His attention slid to the major who stood tense behind her.

"A word, Nikolai." Major Montgomery's low voice rumbled behind her.

The two gentlemen moved to the far side of the car and sat at the table nestled in the corner.

A wave of relief washed over her. At least she would not have to sit through an entire meal in silence with him glowering at her. He behaved as though she did something unforgivable. She pushed the irritation away and turned instead to her newfound friend.

"Come, I have only just ordered my food." Gertrude waved to the waiter.

He stopped beside the table. "*Oui*, madam?"

"Soup and tea, please. *Merci.*"

The waiter nodded and left.

Matilda hesitated to engage her companion in conversation until she knew they would not be overheard.

"Is something troubling you?" Gertrude's kind blue eyes softened before drifting to the two gentlemen in the corner.

"Oh, Gertrude, I seem to have made a muddle of everything." She launched into a brief explanation of her history with Major Montgomery and her affection for the gentleman. She spoke of her confession and his brusque dismissal but refrained from revealing her rash attempt to trick him by ransacking her room.

Gertrude sat with rapt attention, interrupting only momentarily to ask questions or offer words of understanding. When Matilda's emotional tale came to an end, Gertrude sat wide-eyed with her tea cup poised a breath from her lips. She took a fortifying sip as Matilda lapsed into silence.

"I am at a loss." Matilda sighed. "Perhaps I should admit defeat and return home. It is obvious he has no affection for me in the same way that I hold for him."

"I would not discount that yet, *liebling*." Gertrude glanced toward the far side of the dining car.

Matilda glanced behind her and found the major's attention centered on her, not on his companion. He held her gaze for a heartbeat and then turned back toward Mr. Voronia. A flutter of hope beat in her chest.

"If I might make an observation?" Gertrude set her teacup aside.

"Of course." Matilda nearly cried in relief. "I am desperate for advice."

"It seems the major is also trapped in a deep internal struggle. If his letter truly bore his heart, then one can see the conflict." She paused, searching for the right words. "You are young, *liebling*. He may wish to protect you in his own way. Perhaps he believes you deserve a love as youthful and full of optimism as you are."

Matilda shook her head. "I have tried to find love elsewhere, but no man can compare with the major. I love him."

"I understand." Gertrude lay her hand on Matilda's. "Would your parents approve of your choice of husband?"

She glanced out the window. The expansive vineyards passed by in a blur. The mountains rose in the distance. "I do not know. Papa and the major were friends since before I was born. I would hope Papa would understand and wish us every happiness."

"Does it concern you he may not condone such a union?"

"The thought never came into my mind. But after receiving such a forceful rejection from the major, yes, I am concerned my parents may overreact at the prospect of the major and I being together."

Gertrude nodded in sympathy. "I too know what it is like to pine for something forbidden." Sadness filled her gaze as it moved toward the men once more. She shook her head and took Matilda's hand between her own, her eyes brightening.

Before Matilda could ask if she was referring to Mr. Voronia, Gertrude continued, "If you truly wish to capture his heart completely, then he must see the light you bring into his life. Let him see the lovely woman you have become. With a man such as the major, perhaps emphasizing your strengths and displaying your maturity will cause him to reevaluate his position." She lowered her voice. "Make no mistake, the man harbors emotions for you whether he admits them or not."

"How can you possibly know with such certainty?"

"I am well past my prime, *liebling*, but I am not blind. He loves you. You just need him to seize the opportunity that has been placed before him, or he will lose you forever." Her eyes misted at the words before she shook her head and dabbed the corners of her eyes with the linen cloth.

"Mr. Voronia?"

Gertrude nodded. "Yes, but there are other factors which are not so easy to overcome as yours." She smiled, masking all signs of sadness. "Nevermind that. It shall come to right at some point."

Their conversation strayed into more neutral subjects like Gertrude's adept needlepoint skills and their mutual love of gothic tales. A sense of confidence infused her at the words of wisdom offered by her new friend. Matilda's mind churned the conversation over and over, searching for some clue to set her on the path toward a resolution.

In the midst of such a pivotal moment in her life, it helped to know she found an ally and a friend. She only wished it was the major.

CHAPTER THIRTEEN

Anson shifted in his seat opposite Nikolai enough to ensure Matilda remained in his line of sight. Her presence drove him near the point of insanity. Her words clung to the back of his mind. A confession so sweet, so desperate he nearly abandoned all remaining restraint. He forced distance between them. If he spent one more moment alone in her presence, he would do something foolish. Even the short walk down the corridor created conflict in his mind. He smoothed his hand over his thigh and glanced at his companion.

Nikolai smirked and lifted his cup to his lips. His silent judgement infuriated Anson further, if that were possible.

"You wished to speak with me?" Nikolai broke the tension between them.

"After you wipe that look from your face." He growled under his breath.

Nikolai set the cup aside and motioned for him to continue.

Irritation nagged him in equal measure about Matilda and the earlier state of his compartment. He dared not tip his hand to Nikolai, but he required information only the Russian could provide.

"Why were you in Paris?" Anson allowed his direct nature to get the better of him.

Nikolai's brow arched almost imperceptibly as he studied Anson. "The countess requested my services to ensure safe passage to and from Paris since her husband could not accompany her."

"Where is he?"

"He remained in Vienna." Nikolai held his gaze, steady and unyielding.

"Why Paris?"

"An invitation from one of her many friends to indulge in the opera and the ballet." He smirked. "I paid little attention to the productions. I am too occupied watching the crowd." Nikolai's gaze flickered in the direction of Matilda and the countess' traveling companion.

Anson noticed the slight fracture in his friend's otherwise flawless façade. But he made no mention of it. "You pride yourself in your ability to protect your benefactor, yes?"

Nikolai tilted his head in reply.

"You have taken account of every passenger on this train, as well as the railway employees, I gather." He hoped by this point Nikolai will have pieced together the questions and gathered the true meaning of their discussion.

"Of course." Nikolai leaned forward. A spark of curiosity ignited in his bright jade eyes.

"Anything suspicious?"

"Nothing obvious." The Russian steepled his hands and tapped his index fingers together. "Why? What were you doing in Paris?"

"Paying a visit to an old friend." Anson spoke the truth, at least in part. There had been more to his trip than simply socializing. Of course, he could not tell Nikolai the true nature of his journey. The devil lay in the details as they say. While he did not trust Nikolai completely, he proved the only ally who garnered nearly as much experience in espionage and politics as himself. Even though they found themselves on opposite sides of the table on more than one occasion. But it was never personal distaste, only political alliance, that drove a wedge between them.

"And how does she fit into your story?" Nikolai's eyes gleamed.

"Merely a momentary inconvenience." Anson ground his teeth on the last syllable.

"She looks barely a day over nineteen." He glanced between her and Anson twice. "And I know for certain you are nearing fifty."

"She is twenty-one." Anson growled. "And I shall have you

know I have several years until I reach fifty. Not that either of our ages really matter, because there is nothing between us."

"If you say so." Nikolai raised his hands in supplication. "Whatever happened to that enchanting Italian widow I saw you with several months ago at the archduke's gala?"

"*Signora* Castellan—" Anson chose his words with care "—is a vivacious, persistent woman. But I am not interested in tying myself down to a woman who has more political ambitions than myself."

Nikolai nodded, yet a smile played upon his lips.

"If you happen across anything unusual before we arrive in Vienna, notify me immediately."

"Are you afraid *Signora* Castellan has somehow discovered your youthful companion?"

Anson shook his head. "Impossible. And if *Signora* Castellan has set her design upon me, well, I fear she is in for only disappointment."

Nikolai's expression sobered. "And the sweet, young lady in your care? Is she destined only for disappointment as well?"

He resisted the urge to glance at Matilda and ignored Nikolai's penetrating gaze. Her laughter echoed in the dining car. He pinched his eyes closed.

"Perhaps you should not dismiss her so quickly." Nikolai dropped his voice to a soft murmur. "I have known you a long time, my friend, and I have never seen you in this much torment over a woman."

As much as he wanted to indulge in a witty retort, Anson found the way in which he shared the observation to be more out of friendly concern rather than an opponent's jibe.

"Her father is my best friend. What kind of man would I be if I stole away his daughter and kept her for my own pleasure?" Anson shifted in his seat. "What horrid punishments await me in hell for breaking such a bond and ensnaring his innocent daughter in a web of wicked passion?" The words broke from his lips unbidden, unchecked. He hid his face behind his hand. The words sounded even more vile spoken aloud. They stung his ears, and shame buffeted him.

A tense silence fell between them. Anson stared out the window at the snow-covered mountains in the distance. Soon they would cross into Switzerland and deep into the heart of the Alps and then onto Vienna. He would face the stark reality of his betrayal when he contacted his dearest friend concerning the return of his daughter.

"You see yourself the villain in this piece, attempting to steal something bright and wholesome with purely selfish intentions?"

Anson glanced at his companion.

"It is obvious you love her, and that could easily make you the hero of this tale." Nikolai narrowed his gaze. "Unless you break her heart, then a villain you will truly become."

He scoffed. "Love is not so simple."

A dark shadow fell across Nikolai's face, and he frowned, suddenly pensive. "On that, we can agree."

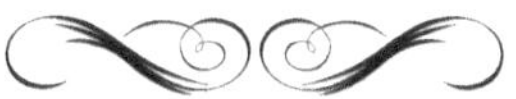

Later in the evening, after a silent dinner with a brooding companion, Matilda retired to her compartment, longing for the comfort of her bed and her favorite book. She swayed at the slow climb of the train through the Alps.

Earlier, her heart soared at the sight of them in the distance. Since the major refused to respond to any of her attempts at civil conversation at supper, she turned her attention to the passing scenery and noted the shadowed mountains glinting with snow in the burgeoning moonlight.

The picturesque view eased the bitter resentment coursing through her. The major, while proving to be an immovable cad, refused to let her out of his sight all day. Even though she wanted to spend time with him, this was not at all how she imagined their adventure together.

After donning her nightgown, Matilda hung her black gown in the small closet and neatly tucked her folded undergarments into her suitcase. Once she tended her toilette and unbound her riotous hair, Matilda curled onto the narrow bed and pulled her book open.

Even her favorite work of fiction was not enough to keep Matilda from falling asleep and dreaming of the handsome man who occupied her thoughts since she was ten.

Matilda woke with a jolt as the train swayed on the tracks. The earsplitting squeal of the brakes echoed in the darkness. Her lamp slid from the table and shattered on the floor. Another bracing jolt shook the train before it slid to a stop.

With her heart racing, Matilda rose from her bed, careful to avoid the pieces of the broken lamp strewn across her floor. A thunderous knock echoed in her compartment.

"Matilda!" The major's harried voice echoed through the door. "Matilda, open the door."

She skirted the edge of the room. A stray shard of glass pierced the sole of her foot. Pain shot up her leg. Careful of her injury, she reached the door and unlocked it.

It slid open under her hand, and Anson's shadow filled the doorway. He wrapped his arms around her.

"Are you all right?" He smoothed his hands over her hair and shoulders.

She basked in the warmth and attention. His spicy scent teased her senses, and her frenzied heartbeat slowed. Even the pain in her foot eased at the comfort of his presence. "I am now." She glanced up at him. "What happened?"

"Felt like an avalanche." He frowned and pulled the watch from his pocket. "We have been climbing the alps all night. It is nearly four in the morning. We must be between Zurich and Innsbruck. Come with me."

He led her from her compartment. She limped with the first step. Anson frowned down at her bare feet.

"What happened to your foot?"

"Oh, well, the lamp shattered when the train…I stepped on some broken glass." Heat suffused her face at the admission.

Without a word, Anson swept her into his arms. She squealed in surprise, and her left hand clung to the front of his unbuttoned shirt. Her thumb brushed his bare chest and warmth blossomed deep into the pit of her stomach. He hesitated for a moment, his grip tightening, and pressed her firmly against his chest before crossing the short distance to his compartment and setting her on his bed.

He wrapped a towel around her injured foot and stood once more.

"Do not move. I shall return in a moment." He bolted from the room, leaving her bewildered and impatient with an odd flutter pulsing beneath her heart.

Her foot ached. She braced herself against the bed to position herself more comfortably. The soft material beneath her fingertips captured her attention. His bed lay mussed, the blankets thrown back, baring the white linens beneath. She ran her fingers across his pillow following the smooth indentation where his head lay while he slumbered. Warmth still permeated the pillow. She jerked her hand away as though it burned her.

The realization of her situation slammed into her with the same force the snow hit the train. It sent her reeling. She sat in his compartment, on his bed. In her nightgown.

Her faced burned with heat, and desire fluttered in her belly. She tried to trick him into this exact moment, and even though her plan failed, it seemed fate decided to grace her with a similar opportunity.

Seduce him, fate whispered.

Matilda shook her head vehemently. Her foot throbbed, and she hissed a breath through her teeth. The desire to curl up in his bed tempted her with a ferocity she could not understand. And yet she waited, patiently, like the good girl he expected. But a wild wantonness called from the dark reaches of her soul.

Her hand skimmed across the warm pillow once more. She leaned down and placed her cheek upon it. The overpowering scent of him sent a pang of longing through her like a streak of lightning across the sky. She closed her eyes and inhaled deeply.

Footsteps echoed in the corridor. Matilda sat up quickly and bumped her foot on the table beside the bed.

"Goddamn it!" She hissed as the pain ricochet through her foot and up her leg.

A masculine chuckle filled the compartment. She squinted against the light from the hall. Anson stood with a small kit in his hands and a bundle of linen.

"Pardon my language, but it hurts!" She pouted, and all thoughts of seduction flew from her mind at the pain.

He set the kit and the clean linens on the bed beside her before retreating into the small shared bathroom in the hall. Anson returned brandishing a wet cloth. He knelt before her and took her ankle in his hands. Carefully, he unwrapped the towel and set it aside.

Matilda's breath caught at the pressure of his fingers against her bare skin. He lifted her foot, tilting it to examine the place where the glass cut. She smiled at his focused expression. Finally, he met her gaze.

"There is still a piece of glass embedded in your foot." He let his thumb trace over the hollow of her ankle. "I need to remove it."

A gasp escaped Matilda before she could stop it. His touch burned her sensibility and left it lying in ashes on the floor. She nodded, unable to trust herself to form coherent words.

"It will be fine. It is a small piece," he soothed her. Then, without warning, he pulled the shard from the pad of her foot.

"Son of a bi—scuit!" Matilda swore, shifting words mid-sentence, aware of his silent gaze upon her.

Anson set the bloody shard aside and pressed the cool cloth to the bottom of her foot, applying pressure upon the wound.

Matilda bit her lip to keep from crying out as the pain tore through her. Stars swam before her eyes briefly before the warm, comforting pressure of Anson's hands gently massaged away the stinging agony. She drew her lower lip between her teeth and whimpered.

Anson glanced up from where he knelt before her, his hands hidden beneath the hem of her nightgown, wrapped around her injured foot. The poor lighting played tricks. His eyes darkened three shades, turning from the calm blue sea into the vibrant haze of a summer storm.

She opened her mouth, but words refused to come. What if she spoke and the moment shattered? What if he pushed her away, again? Her heart could not take another bout with him.

Silence lingered between them as he reached for the kit and the linens. Aware of her tender injury, he cleaned the wound, placed some salve on it, and wrapped it. His careful ministrations showed attention to detail, but also no rush on his part.

"What happened to the train?" She attempted to focus the attention on something other than the way he touched her and how much she enjoyed it.

"Avalanche, as I suspected." He secured the first bandage and wound another around her foot. "The train is stuck. They will have to dig us out. The porter told me they sent men to the nearest village to find help to expedite the process."

"How far is the village?"

"A few miles back. They should return before morning and have the train freed by tomorrow evening, if all goes well." He tied the linen and released her foot.

"Can you bear my company for an extra day?" A keen sense of loss settled over her as he pulled away and rose to his feet.

"I believe I can endure your company for a while longer." He set the towels in the corridor along with the kit and closed the door.

"What are you doing?" Her heart thrashed against her ribs when he stood beside her, his leg brushing her thigh.

He lowered the bunk above his bed and glanced down. "The porter cannot clean your cabin until tomorrow. It would be better for you to spend the night here rather than hazard another shard of glass in your foot."

Disappointment rankled her yet again. "Of course." She tried to rise, so she could climb into the top bunk, but the moment she placed her foot on the floor, pain radiated through her.

"What are you doing?" He placed his hands on her shoulders and pushed her down once more. "You can sleep there. I shall take the top bunk. It is only for one night."

"Are you certain?" His hands on her shoulders provided the comfort she desired.

"I believe I can manage." He released her.

"Major Montgomery."

"I believe we have progressed beyond the pleasantries, Matilda." He smiled. "Call me Anson."

"Thank you, Anson." She twisted the fabric of her nightgown between her fingers. "For coming to my aid and bandaging my foot."

"Of course." He cupped her chin in his hand, tilting her face up until their eyes met. "Please accept my apology. I behaved horribly these past two days, and well, if I am honest, the past year. We find ourselves caught up in something neither of us expected, and I handled it poorly. Can you forgive me?"

Tears welled in her eyes. The pain of her injured foot did not cause a single tear, and yet Anson's apology tore open the wounds she hid for the past year. She sniffed, trying to hold back the torrent of emotion.

"You must think I am foolish, chasing after you like some lovesick puppy."

"I never once thought of you as foolish." He took her hand in his, and her heart leapt at the contact. "You were a child. Every letter, every exchange, I saw the headstrong, adventurous ten-year-old girl who met me at her father's front door demanding adventure."

She chuckled, and a tear slipped down her cheek.

Anson wiped it away with his thumb, which lingered against her cheek for a moment before brushing against the corner of her mouth as his hand fell away. "But you are not a child anymore. I see that now, and it terrifies me."

Her heart stopped, and yet she pressed forward hoping against hope. "I terrify you?"

He shook his head. "The things you make me feel."

"How do I make you feel?"

He leaned closer. "Like a man standing in the midst of a thunderstorm. The wind raging, the rain pouring, the thunder and lightning surging. Common sense tells me to seek shelter from the tempest, and yet all I want is to be swept away by its beauty."

Tears spilled forth once more. Matilda swiped them away with her hand. "Why are you telling me this?"

"Because, you deserve to know what a rare gem you are. I am not worthy of such a treasure. You deserve better."

"I deserve better?" As she repeated his words, they soured on her tongue. "You are right, Anson. I do deserve better." Fury infused her, spreading through her body like wildfire. She pulled away from him.

He frowned.

"I deserve a man who knows exactly what he wants and is not afraid take it." She turned away and flopped down onto his bed with her back toward him, pulling the blankets up over her body. "Good night."

Matilda stared at the wall until Anson extinguished the light and climbed into the bunk above her. His oblivious denial infuriated her more than anything. She poured her heart out, and still he maintained his position that she deserved better. Even when he seemed so close to realizing the truth himself.

CHAPTER FOURTEEN

On the Alpine Express
November 16, 1899

Anson lay in the dark and stared at the ceiling. Regret coursed through him mingled with a current of restless energy which only compounded in Matilda's presence.

Her occupying his bed did not soothe his conscience when it came to her safety.

He made a valiant attempt to be a gentleman and failed spectacularly. He had been close, so close to confessing, to bearing his soul to the woman who haunted not only his waking moments but his dreams. He lifted his arm over his head and flexed his fingers.

There was little he could do except dwell on the events leading to this point. That knowledge irritated him beyond measure.

When the abrupt stop of the train and the impact of the avalanche woke him, his first reaction was to seek out Matilda and ensure her safety. Finding her dressed only her nightgown, hair tousled from sleep, threw his mind into chaos and his body into desperate need. Her injury unleashed a beast inside him demanding he protect her.

How foolish could he possibly be? After his conversation with Nikolai, he found himself even more irritated with the situation. Dinner proved disastrous. He could not engage in basic polite conversation. His attention strayed from his own meal to her lips as she ate, the soft curve of her hand holding the fork, and the longing painted on her face when she saw the mountains coming closer with every passing moment.

Anson always believed he possessed strength and moral

integrity, yet the time spent with Matilda challenged his convictions. Her smile and laughter, her mere presence, chipped away at his resolve.

He cringed and hid his eyes beneath his forearm. The heartfelt apology spilled from him in a moment of pure honesty. And yet, what came after turned the sweet moment into a catastrophic disaster. He groaned at his own inability to communicate.

What was he trying to say? Even he found himself perplexed by the words pouring from his lips. He had been a heartbeat from kissing her. But as if confounded by his own conscience, his mind stepped in and seized everything in a hasty retreat.

Hurt flashed in her tear-filled eyes, imprinting on his memory like a brand searing into flesh. He cursed himself for being lower than a cad.

Irritated and unable to sleep, Anson climbed from the upper bunk and dressed, careful not to wake her. Daybreak peeked through the curtains. Perhaps if he volunteered his services to free the train, it would serve dual purposes, both to clear his body of the pent-up energy and ensure their timely arrival in Vienna.

He must send a telegram to Jacob once they reached Salzburg station. At the very least, his friend should know that his daughter was safe and would return home as soon as possible.

He fixed his jacket with a firm tug and buttoned it. The soft rise and fall of the blanket belied her slumbering state. He shook his head. One of them would be well-rested at least.

Once he slipped from the compartment, Anson locked the door behind him and set off down the corridor in search of the porter. He slowly made his way to the tail of the train where the baggage compartment door stood open.

He slid open the connecting door and stepped through the cold to enter the baggage car. Inside, he stopped. Two men struggled with a large trunk.

"Good morning." Anson's gaze shifted over the scene.

One of the men dropped the trunk and turned.

Neither men were employees of the railway. Both men were

in the dining car the day before. With a tilt of his head, Anson remained polite. "Has either of you seen the porter?"

"You think I would be here shuffling through the baggage car looking for my luggage if I knew where the porter was?" The man's attitude set Anson on edge.

"They are all removing the snow." His companion pointed toward the window. His accent sounded different from the first, but unmistakably Italian.

"Oh, well that certainly helps. Thank you." Anson ignored second man's scowl and the first's narrowed gaze. "Good luck with your luggage." He turned without waiting for a response.

Once surrounded by the warmth of the sleeping car, he leaned against the wall and watched the men through the small glass window. They shifted the trunk and removed other items from the rack. When they opened one, Anson frowned. They were looking for something, and it was not a misplaced bag.

Who were they? He knew for certain one of them was Italian, the other proved to be a bit more complex. French? Perhaps closer to the Italian border with France? He waited a few moments and watched them sort through several more pieces. They pushed the last trunk aside with irritation.

Their animated movements revealed an unsuccessful search. Anson rubbed his jaw and hurried down the corridor before they returned to the main compartments. He did not wish to meet them again in such an isolated environment. He hurried through the three sleeping cars and paused inside the lounge car. Nikolai abandoned his view of the snow-covered valley and glanced up.

"*Dobroye utro.*" Nikolai greeted him with a tilt of his head. He sipped his coffee and returned his gaze to the scene outside.

"Good morning to you too." Anson sat beside him and glanced around.

"The waiter is in the dining car." The light played on Nikolai's face, illuminating the dark shadows beneath his reddened eyes.

"You look terrible. Trouble sleeping?"

Nikolai turned, his expression inscrutable, like a glacier

frosted by the icy wind. "As do you, my friend."

Anson sighed and crossed his arms. "What do you know about those two men traveling together?"

His companion arched his brow. "You do not recognize them?"

Unease settled over Anson. "You do?"

"Of course, it took me until after dinner last evening to remember where I saw them before." Nikolai took a drink. "They belong to the Italian widow."

"*Signora* Castellan?" Anson sat up. His mind raced.

Nikolai nodded.

"What are they doing here?"

The Russian shrugged. "Holiday in Paris."

"I do not believe it is coincidence. Two of her men in Paris returning on the same train as me." Anson visualized the two men searching the baggage car. "They are looking for something."

Nikolai narrowed his gaze. "Explain, please."

Anson relayed his observations in the baggage car and the state in which he found his compartment the day before.

Nikolai shook his head. "You did not trust me with this information yesterday? You wound me." He pressed his hand to his heart.

"Would you have trusted me so easily?"

A smile broke upon the Russian's face. "After all these years, I would hope our friendship would be stronger than our politics."

"Perhaps one day it may be. Right now, I require your assistance."

"Who do you want me to kill?"

"Nothing so extreme." Anson smiled at the half-serious but typical humor. "I must send a telegram once we reach Salzburg. Matilda must not leave the train while I am gone. Can I entrust her to your care?"

"Of course, my friend."

Anson found Nikolai's quick response unnerving. The Russian often required something in exchange for his cooperation. He eyed the man beside him and wondered if he did not just play into his hands.

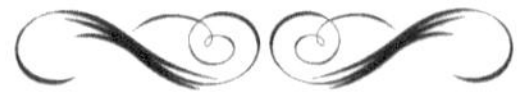

The icy glass cooled her warm skin. She pressed her face harder against the window, as though it would grant her the ability to see the train from the outside. Curiosity burned inside her.

Matilda woke alone, which she found preferable since her embarrassment did not diminish with sleep. Her face burned at the memory of her foolish behavior. Anson showed no change of heart. The apology simply eased his own conscience.

She exhaled against the frosted pane and drew a lopsided heart on the fogged glass. Her eyes drifted closed. Was she naïve enough to think she could change his mind in a few short hours?

Obviously, she believed it possible, or she never would have run away from her parents in the dead of night and bought a one-way passage on the Alpine Express. She longed for adventure and romance. Anson could offer her both. Instead, he shattered her dreams at every opportunity.

With a groan, Matilda smeared the heart from the glass with her palm and turned away from the window. She gently stood and hobbled across the room, keeping the weight off her bandaged foot. The door latch refused to budge. She shook the door and slammed her fist against it.

Of course, it did not magically unlock in the time since she last checked. When she found herself locked in his room, she raged against the injustice of it, beating her fists against the pillow. She was sorely tempted to upend his suitcase out of spite.

This time, she collapsed on the bed in defeat. When he returned, he would certainly be on the receiving end of her ire.

Matilda could still feel his warm hands on her ankle and see the dark hunger swimming in the depths of his piercing eyes. She squirmed uncomfortably at the memories. How he lifted her so easily and carried her into his compartment. The way he stiffened beneath the innocent brush of her fingertips against his chest.

The breath she held waiting for him to kiss her.

Only for the moment to die with that horrid phrase. *You deserve better.* Those words repelled her in the way discovering a rotting corpse in her bed might. She shivered with disgust.

Why did he persist in pushing her away? Another woman? Matilda shook her head. No, surely after last night, after his apology, there could be no one else. But who could possibly know for certain?

Her father? No, he never mentioned anything about Anson and a woman. They were best friends for years and kept in constant correspondence. If there were a woman, her father would have mentioned it, even in passing. What of his Russian friend, Mr. Voronia? Gertrude mentioned their close friendship during luncheon the day before, perhaps he knew something. But how in the devil could she approach him?

Matilda chewed her lip in frustration. Well, she could not do anything until he released her from her prison, even dress properly. She glanced down at the nightgown. The material kept her warm, but being locked away made her overly warm. She unbuttoned the gown and pressed her cool hand against her chest. A bit of the tension eased.

Thoughts of Anson brought the heat flooding back in waves. Both her anger and her undeniable attraction served as a firm reminder of her situation.

The door clicked as the lock turned. Matilda sat up and pressed a hand to her throat. The door slid open.

Anson stepped inside the room bearing a tray. After latching the door behind him, he placed the tray laden with breakfast upon the table beside the bed.

"I did not think you would be up to walking to the dining car for breakfast." He made an admirable attempt at sounding civil. "Your foot probably hurts like hell."

"It is quite tender." Her gaze drifted to the eggs, bacon, coffee, and croissant sitting neatly on the table. Her traitor of a stomach gurgled with hunger.

"Eat, before it gets cold." He pulled out the chair next to the desk and sat down. His presence dominated the space.

Warmth spread through her. "Must you always make demands?" She pulled the napkin from the tray and lay it across her lap. "You are worse than my father." The words tumbled from her tongue before she truly thought of the implications they may incur. Her hand trembled above the fork. She lifted her gaze to Anson.

His brilliant gaze sparkled in the morning light. Arms crossed, he sat with a regal bearing and watched her. His expression remained impassive.

"I apologize." She leaned over the plate to take a bite of eggs. The rich velvety texture melted upon her tongue. She sighed in pleasure. Her gaze drifted back to him.

His arched brow framed those hungry eyes. A more controlled hunger, but still present. Without a word, he retreated from the room. Disappointment raged through her. Could she ever do anything right?

Before she could dwell upon it, he returned with an armful of her clothes and her suitcase in his hand. He dumped the pile beside her on the bed.

He closed the door and resumed his seat.

"Would you care for some?" Matilda struggled to keep her voice from shaking.

"I have already eaten." His brusque response irritated her.

Her mouth full, she dropped the fork on the plate. The clatter punctuated the silence between them.

"Will you please tell me what I have done to offend you?" Frustration coiled inside her. She bore his cold indifference the day before, but today, it seemed he wished to continue in the same manner. Even after his apology. Matilda refused to bear it a moment longer.

"Now what would lead you believe you have offended me?" He maintained a calm tone.

"You treat me like an unwanted burden one moment, and in the next, you tend my wounds and protect my honor as though I were the most precious thing in the world." She searched his face for any hint of reaction. The stoic demeanor she once thought attractive now drove her insane. "Once again

I am the unwanted burden." Matilda shoved the plate away.

"What an astute observation." His mouth pulled to one side in a sarcastic smile and stood. "Once you have dressed, you may return to your compartment. The porter is cleaning it now."

Anger flared and raged through her entire body. "I will not be treated in such a manner. You are not my father. Nor are you in any position to tell me what to do. I release you from your honor bound responsibilities." She rose to her feet. "I can take care of myself."

Anson crossed the room faster than she could take a breath. His broad body blocked her against the bed. She twisted her neck to glare at him. The handsome cad with those piercing eyes and stubble covered jaw stole the air from the room. She licked her lips. Her sudden bravado disappeared faster than snow in July.

"Enough, Matilda. That is quite enough."

His heady scent wrapped around her, the mint on his breath teased her. She blinked up at him.

"Until we reach your parent's door, you are under my protection, and that means you will do as I instruct you." He braced his hands on the upper bunk, framing the side of her head and pinning her still. "This is the final time we will have this conversation. Do you understand?"

Matilda could only glare. His command infuriated her, yet deep in the recesses of her mind, she longed for this. For him to take control. A battle waged recklessly inside her. She pressed her lips together and shook her head.

"If you defy me, I will treat you exactly the way a father would treat a disobedient child." His eyes darkened, and they focused on her mouth when it dropped open.

"What will you do?" Her heart pounded.

He did not respond to her question, but she saw the promise of retribution in his expression as he pulled away. "Get dressed. I will return to escort to your compartment."

"No, please." She bit her lip when he paused, keeping his back to her. "I would rather sit in the lounge."

Anson glanced over his shoulder. "Very well." With those words, he left and locked the door behind him.

Matilda collapsed on the bed. Her heart raced, and she struggled to catch her breath. What in the Lord's name just happened? She pressed her hand to her chest against the heat of her skin. She glanced down. Her nightgown remained unbuttoned. Anson must have seen more than he expected while she ate breakfast.

Shame flooded her, but it dissipated into a heady arousal. Did she still wish to seduce him? Of course. His bold words betrayed him. He wanted her, but if she was to succeed, she would need guidance.

Matilda prayed Gertrude would be in the lounge car. If anything, she needed the advice of a woman who knew the ways of the world more intimately than she.

CHAPTER FIFTEEN

Matilda and Gertrude occupied a cozy, warm spot in the corner of the vacant lounge car. The window provided an uninhibited view of the snow-covered valley below. Tucked beneath a warm blanket, Matilda propped her foot on a small stool and ordered tea from the waiter.

Anson spoke very little following their confrontation in his compartment. With his aid, she limped down the corridor to the lounge car. Her foot protested at the prolonged use. But Matilda refused to remain trapped in the sleeping car all day.

His threat of punishment weighted on her mind. A small thrill coursed through her at the thought of him lavishing her with any attention, even a reprimand. Part of her longed to misbehave if it fed her hunger. She sighed in frustration.

"His affections have not been swayed, *liebling?*" Gertrude shifted in the seat opposite her.

Matilda glanced at the door where Anson disappeared moments before. "No, they have not." Her gaze focused upon her companion. "Last evening, I injured my foot. He came to my aid and carried me to his compartment where he tended to the wound. I could have sworn there was a moment when he would profess his love." She frowned and shrugged.

"Men are strange creatures." Gertrude smiled in sympathy. "I do not understand them any more than you do, even though I am ten years your senior."

"Surely you have learned something of the ways of men." Matilda grasped the opening in the conversation.

Gertrude's face flushed a delightful shade of pink, and she waved her hand. "I have no such knowledge. In fact, I believe I am as innocent as yourself in such regards."

Matilda slumped in her chair with disappointment. "I know

only of the heartache sown by rejection."

"That makes two of us."

The waiter appeared with their tray bearing tea and sandwiches.

"*Merci.*" Matilda thanked him.

The waiter left them in peace once more.

As Gertrude prepared the tea, Matilda studied her. The golden tresses she envied wound in a halo braid around the crown of Gertrude's head. She wore a simple dirndl gown, in traditional Bavarian style, with soft blue and silver accents. It complimented the surrounding décor of the lounge car with its rich blue and gold brocade against the mahogany panels.

"Here, this should warm you." Gertrude passed her the cup and saucer.

"*Danke schon.*" The steaming beverage soothed her throat. Warmth and contentment, perhaps the first true contentment in days, settled over her. Matilda relaxed and her gaze roamed the snowcapped peaks beyond the glass.

"How did your acquaintance with the major begin?" Gertrude lifted the cup to her lips. Her blue eyes rested curiously on Matilda.

"Well." Her cheeks burned at Gertrude's curious question. "My father and the major served together in Her Majesty's Royal Army. My father married my mother and took up work for Parliament. The major remained in service until he, well I am unsure why he decided to leave the military."

"How interesting." Gertrude's eyes sparkled.

"I met him on my tenth birthday. He dined at our home in London before he left England as a liaison for the embassy in France." She warmed at the memory. "He presented me with a sketch of Versailles and promised me gifts from every city he visited."

Gertrude smiled.

"We corresponded for years. We have a mutual love of travel, you see, and discussed all of the places he visited in his years abroad." Her heart twisted at the memory of their innocent exchanges. "Until I became engaged."

The tea cup clattered against the plate as Gertrude fumbled with the cup in her hand. "Engaged?" Confusion marred her brow. "You were engaged?"

"I was." Matilda struggled with the lingering bitterness. "A handsome gentleman asked me to marry him. He was well-connected and from a wealthy family. Yet, the engagement dissolved two years later."

"Oh, *liebling*, how awful." Gertrude set her cup aside and reached for Matilda's hand, giving it a loving squeeze.

"At first, I was despondent. I could not eat. I could not sleep. I rarely left my bedchamber." Matilda sighed. "Then I realized, I was not heartsick over the loss of my engagement or my betrothed."

Realization lit Gertrude's face. "The major."

Matilda nodded. "I harbored a tendre for him for years. Since the moment I first saw him. Being a child, it hardly seemed relevant. Who would believe such an infatuation would last so long?" She lifted a shoulder. "After my broken engagement, I wrote him a very different letter."

"And you poured your heart into it?" Gertrude seemed riveted by the tale.

"I did." Matilda paused. "His response took some time to reach me, and when it did, it gave me hope, as if the stars aligned, bringing us together in a perfect moment."

"What happened?" Gertrude leaned forward, eager for the story to unfold.

"Months passed, and I heard nothing from him until my birthday, when I received a note which read *Happy Birthday*."

Gertrude's mouth dropped open. "How could he...I do not understand." She offered an apologetic shake of her head. "*Mein liebling.*"

"I continued writing and prayed for a reply. Something. Months passed without a word." Matilda sighed. "I lost hope, until we accompanied my father on his business errand to Paris. I did not realize Major Montgomery would make an appearance, until he joined us for my birthday dinner."

"This was the first time you saw him since you first met?"

"Yes." Matilda laughed at the absurdity it all. "Am I insane? To love a man I met on only two occasions? A man twice my age, old enough to be my father? A man dedicated to his country."

"We cannot choose the ones we love." Gertrude held her hand.

"He told me I deserve better."

"You do." Her response startled Matilda. Gertrude's eyes shone with sympathy. "We both do." She gave Matilda's hand a firm squeeze.

"I still love him. I cannot help the way I feel."

"I understand, *liebling*."

Matilda shook her head. "The worst part of it all…when I injured my foot, and he rescued me."

Gertrude nodded.

"I thought I saw it." She chewed on her lower lip. "The hunger in his gaze. It felt as though he wanted to kiss me and refrained. Perhaps I am imagining such things."

"If you saw the hunger there, why did you not act upon it?"

Matilda cocked her head in surprise. "Why would I act upon it?"

"Did you want him to kiss you?"

"More than anything."

"Yet he did not."

"No." Matilda frowned. "But I want him to kiss me. How can I convince him to kiss me?"

Gertrude laughed. "You cannot convince a man to do anything."

"Then what should I do?"

"Kiss him first."

Matilda blinked, stunned by the revelation. Could the solution be so simple? "Kiss him?"

"Yes, *liebling*. Show him how you feel through actions, not words."

As though a revelation by a choir of angels, Matilda's mind calmed and her direction became clear. "You are a treasure, my friend." She drew Gertrude close, kissing her on the cheek.

"Thank you."

"Of course." Gertrude laughed. She reached for her bag and drew it into her lap. "Oh no. Where is it?" She rifled through the oversized bag several times before collapsing in defeat.

"Is something the matter?"

"I cannot find my journal." She laughed. "I always write down things so I remember it later when I need it." Gertrude shook her head. "I can never follow my own advice, and lately I find I need all the help I can get. Perhaps I left it in my compartment."

"Well, what does it look like? I shall keep watch for it in case I see it lying on the train."

"It is a small, leather bound journal. Large enough to write comfortably, but small enough to fit in one's pocket. Or in my case, my handbag." She lifted the accessory with a shrug.

"I shall watch for it." Matilda offered her hand.

Gertrude took it with a smile. "*Danke, liebling.* And fret not, I am sure the major will come to his senses soon enough."

"I certainly hope so." For the first time since the night Anson appeared in Paris, Matilda found herself hopeful for the future. She would seduce the major.

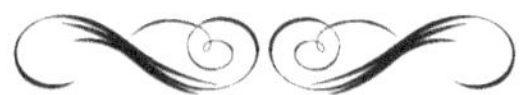

The sun set on the horizon and cast long shadows across the silent valley. Damp with perspiration, Anson leaned his shovel against the side of the train car.

Once he deposited Matilda in the relative safety of the lounge with Nikolai's traveling companion, Gertrude, he volunteered to help dislodge the train from the mound of snow cascading from the mountainside.

The avalanche proved much less dire than he feared. His initial concerns melted once he stepped out into the brisk mountain air and found the workers shoveling snow. A large drift of snow collided with the train, and a little over half of it remained.

He glanced at Nikolai, who worked in only his shirtsleeves,

shoveling with surprising speed for a man of his age.

Anson arched a brow and shook his head. "How are you not frozen?"

Nikolai grinned at him. "You forget. I was born and raised in the heart of Mother Russia. These temperatures are tropical compared to what I experienced as a child." He tossed another shovel full over his shoulder. "Once we return to the warmth of the train, it will be easier for my body to adapt." He pointed to Anson's coat which hung open. "You will see."

Darkness settled around them. The workers sent up a cheer as the last of the snow shifted beneath the train cars. Anson and Nikolai returned their equipment and boarded the train. They climbed up the narrow ladder and stepped into the small space connecting the lounge car with the first sleeper car.

The sudden elevation in temperature surged to Anson's head. He stripped his overcoat and suit jacket, which slipped from his hands. Both garments dropped to the floor.

"I warned you." Nikolai retrieved the coats. He brushed off the snow and dirt before handing them to Anson.

He tucked the garments over his arm and gestured to his damp shirt. "I shall join you in a moment."

The train whistle echoed through the night. With a jerk, the steel beast surged into motion once more. Relief flooded him. Hopefully they would reach Salzburg by morning. A twinge of remorse tugged at his heart. He hated knowing his time with Matilda would soon come to an end. It pained him to admit he enjoyed the little time he allowed himself with her.

After he slid the compartment door closed, Anson peeled off his waistcoat and soaked shirt before collapsing on the bed. He took a few moments to rest. The air in the cabin became a cool relief upon his overheated skin.

He splashed some water on his face and took a few minutes to freshen up.

"Much better." He hung the towel on the hook inside the door.

As he pulled on a fresh shirt, he wondered if Matilda enjoyed her afternoon in the lounge. She could not wander far because of her injury. He wondered if he should have the doctor they met the day before look at her wound. In the poor light, it appeared superficial, but one could never be too careful.

Resolved, he buttoned his shirt. When he pulled on his jacket, he patted the inside pocket out of habit. Empty.

A sudden jolt of fear gripped him. His notebook, containing all his meticulous entries, was gone. Did he drop it in the snow outside? He raked his hands through his hair. Surely, he would have seen the dark leather against the pale snow. He ignored donning a tie and checked the corridor where he dropped his coat.

Preoccupied, he burst into the hallway and collided with Fräulein Bleul.

"Oooof." She swayed at the impact.

Anson steadied her with gentle hand on her shoulder. "I apologize. Are you well?" Concerned and embarrassed, he stepped aside, dropping his hand. "Please forgive me. I…well, I have no excuse for my behavior."

"I am well." She clutched her bag to her chest. "Please, think nothing of it." She smiled and her blue eyes sparkled beneath her braided golden crown. "Matilda is waiting for you in the dining car. I must go tend to the countess."

"Yes, well, thank you for entertaining Matilda. She enjoys your company." Anson tipped his head. "Have a lovely evening, Fräulein Bleul."

"You as well, Major Montgomery." Gertrude retreated in the direction of her sleeper car.

With a renewed sense of purpose, Anson returned to the place where he and Nikolai just boarded the train. He searched the area twice and found nothing. His journal vanished.

Anson cursed and returned to his compartment. He searched every conceivable area before conceding defeat. Then he remembered Matilda awaited his company in the dining car.

He swore again. Aware of both failures, he smoothed his hand over his lapels as he strode toward the dining car.

Once he stepped into the lounge car, he glimpsed her red hair through the far door. She was not alone.

Nikolai.

Anson saw the spark of joy in her expression, the sparkle of her green eyes in the lamplight and the pink tinge of color in her cheeks. Her lips parted mid-laughter. Humor reflected in her eyes.

Jealousy caught him like an unexpected right hook, knocking the breath from his chest. He gripped the handle so tightly he thought it would break. Longing gripped his heart. How he wished to be on the receiving end of her laughter, her unbridled joy.

Matilda's gaze fell upon him. The humor faded and her brilliant smile disappeared. Sadness filled her expression before it vanished as though it had never been there. She turned her attention to Nikolai and the brilliance returned.

Pain, white hot, pierced his heart and enveloped the jealousy twisting like serpents in the pit of his stomach. Anson released the door handle and turned his back on the dining car.

Defeated, Anson ordered a double whisky content to drown his misery in the bottle of scotch. He would never be the source of her delight, and that knowledge hung like a noose around his throat.

CHAPTER SIXTEEN

"A room filled with braying donkeys." Mr. Voronia's smile proved infectious. "It took hours to remove them all. The smell lingers still on damp nights."

Matilda laughed until her sides ached. The pain in her foot and her heart eased at the levity of the moment. After spending much of the day with Gertrude discussing their love of gothic literature and the agony of unrequited love, the sudden shift in companionship created a welcome change.

While she adored Gertrude's company, Matilda harbored a smidge of curiosity when it came to the tall, handsome Russian. His vivid jade eyes betrayed nothing. Composed and eloquent, the man wore secrecy like a shroud, obvious from the first introduction.

With her profound apologies, Gertrude left after the porter delivered an urgent summons from the countess, pulling her from their supper.

Mr. Voronia proved an interesting conversationalist. He never spoke more than necessary and his attention to detail astounded her. He asked where she grew up and what kind of hobbies she enjoyed. He shared a bit of himself as well. She found his description of growing up in St. Petersburg fascinating in comparison to her own upbringing in London.

His tale of the grand duke's seventieth birthday celebration highlighted by the performance of the circus sounded ludicrous. Matilda laughed out loud, allowing herself to enjoy the humor. Etiquette be damned, it brought her such joy to converse freely.

A shadow beyond the compartment door caught her eye. Anson stood framed by the ornate cut glass; his lips pressed in a thin line of displeasure.

Her heartbeat skipped at the sight of him, but all joy fled

when he scowled. Was he still upset with her? She hoped he would join them. But when he did not move, she turned her attention back to Mr. Voronia who sipped his wine.

Matilda lifted her own glass and drank. When her gaze slipped back to the doorway, Anson had vanished.

Mr. Voronia studied her over the crystal rim. "He is a complicated man."

The comment caught her unaware. Matilda shook herself free of her musings. "I beg your pardon."

"Your countenance changed. I assume my old friend finally appeared." He glanced over his shoulder. "I see he chose not to join us."

Matilda waved her hand. "Yes, well. I believe we have reached an impasse. I do not think he desires to be in my company more than he must."

"On the contrary." Mr. Voronia's voice deepened with conviction. "I think he desires it more than he dare admit to anyone, especially himself."

A glint of hope shone in the dark void. Matilda hardly dared to believe it. "He knows my thoughts and feelings when it comes to our relationship, and I know his." She squared her shoulders. "I am only a child with no concept of what I desire. He has made it perfectly clear I have no place in his life."

His astute gaze lingered on her for the space of several heartbeats. She shivered at the blunt appraisal. When he spoke, his voice echoed low between them. "Major Montgomery is the most honorable and patriotic man I have ever met. He has proven himself as both an ally and friend. But when it comes to matters of the heart, he is *durak*." When she blinked in confusion, he clarified. "What you would call an idiot."

Matilda clapped her hand over her mouth and smothered her laughter. Once she calmed, she cleared her throat. "What do you mean?"

"The major has one love." Mr. Voronia leaned back and flexed his fingers together in a steepled movement. "His country."

"I do not understand—" Matilda stopped when Mr.

Voronia laughed.

"*Milyy rebenok.*" His paused, his words soft, and shook his head. "Sweet child. He lives for his work. It has been his passion during all the time I have known him. Never have I seen him look at a woman the way he looks at you."

Heat blossomed across her face. Matilda hid behind her glass of wine. "Mr. Voronia."

"Love is nothing to be ashamed of."

"I have told him of my love."

"Words are not enough to convince a man."

Matilda stared at him. His confidence infused her conviction. "You have a point, Mr. Voronia."

The waiter approached with their dinner upon his silver tray. He placed the roasted pheasant and potatoes before her, and the divine scent made her mouth water even though her hunger diminished thanks to the nervous flutters in her stomach. She sliced a bit of meat and lifted it to her lips. How soon could she excuse herself without appearing rude?

Her anticipation grew with every passing moment. After dinner, she would put advice into practice.

The liquor failed to numb the unrelenting ache in his chest. She sat just beyond the door conversing with the enemy. He shook his head. No, not the enemy. That was unfair to Nikolai. Their history bore more respect than such a brash assessment.

Anson drained the remainder of the liquid in his glass.

He lost his notebook. Anson shook his head and pushed the empty glass away. He lost the woman he cared above all else in the world. Failure surrounded him, dragging him under the dark waters of misery.

"Are you well?" The cultured French accent pulled Anson from his dark reverie.

He glanced to his right. The doctor sat beside him; his bushy eyebrows emphasized the concern in his wide brown eyes. Anson could not recall his name. Doctor Bushybrows? He shook his head free of the scotch's spell.

"Doctor Archer. We met yesterday in the corridor."

"Ah, yes, forgive me, Doctor." He offered his hand. "I am not myself lately." The doctor shook it. "Major Montgomery."

"I quite understand." The gentleman glanced around. "And where is the lovely Mrs. Hudson this evening."

"She is dining with a friend." He nodded toward the dining car.

"I see." Doctor Archer glanced over his spectacles at Anson.

"I hoped to speak with you." Anson filled the awkward void full of unasked questions. "Mrs. Hudson injured her foot last evening. A shard of broken glass. I treated it the best I could, however, I am concerned the cut may require further attention. I am not adept at sutures."

"Of course." Doctor Archer stood immediately. "Shall we see if she is finished with supper? I do not wish to wait for fear of infection."

Anson did not intend to interrupt her dinner with Nikolai, but Dr. Archer dragged him from the barstool and into the dining car.

Matilda glanced up from her plate as they approached. "Good evening, Doctor Archer, Major Montgomery." Her warm welcome for the doctor did not extend to him. The brusque emphasis on his name made him wince. "Would you care to join us?"

Nikolai turned toward Anson, who gave a nearly imperceptive shake of his head. His lip curled in amusement, but he remained silent.

"Thank you, no, Mrs. Hudson. Major Montgomery tells me you have injured your foot. Would you allow me to take a look at it? He voiced his concern it may need further treatment." The doctor's attention focused solely on Matilda.

She flushed at the question. "If you think it is necessary, doctor."

"Very well, shall we retreat to your compartment? I shall have the porter fetch my bag." The doctor strode off to locate the porter in the lounge car.

Matilda rose to her feet and swayed as she placed pressure on her sore foot.

Anson reached for her, but she pulled away from him.

"I am more than capable of walking unassisted, thank you." She turned her attention to Nikolai. "I enjoyed your company and the conversation. If you will pardon me."

Nikolai rose to his feet. "Allow me to escort you to your room. It would not be wise to over exert yourself."

Anson wanted to throttle him. He stepped aside to allow the Russian to offer Matilda his arm.

Beneath the whisky-soaked façade of calm, Anson seethed. Nikolai had always been blunt and brash, perpetually unashamed about speaking his mind, no matter the opinion. It never bothered Anson before, but this did.

She would not allow him to aid her. Her decision to shun him at every possible turn singed his pride. He could hardly blame her given his repeated rejection of her affections. Still, jealousy burned white hot in his veins.

Matilda rested her arm upon Nikolai's and he bore her weight as they walked together from the dining car. The couple in the corner glanced up when the group passed their table.

The doctor held the door for them as they entered the lounge car. He hurried ahead, ensuring easy passage to the sleeper cars.

Anson trailed behind.

The two gentlemen he encountered in the luggage car sat in the corner of the lounge. Cigarettes smoldered between their fingertips. Their gazes narrowed hawk-like upon them as they passed through the carriage. The one with the thick mustache murmured something to his companion.

A wave of unease swept through Anson. He studied them as he passed, noting, much to his distaste, that Nikolai was correct. Both men served at the behest of *Signora* Castellan. What were they doing on this train? And what in the devil were they searching for in the luggage car?

Both men remained impassive. Their attention focused on

the small party as they moved through the lounge.

Anson closed the door behind them. He followed down the corridor and into the next sleeper car where their compartments lay.

"Just in here." Matilda's voice echoed in front of him.

Anson remained in the hallway until Nikolai retreated after depositing her on the edge of her bed.

"Such a gentleman," Anson hissed under his breath when Nikolai joined him.

"At least one of us behaves as such." Nikolai's barb cut sharper than a knife.

Anson flexed his hand into a fist and unfurled his fingers several times. He pushed aside the scathing retort on his tongue and instead glanced at Matilda through the doorway.

"If you let her escape, then I have no sympathy for the painful existence you will lead." Nikolai leaned close to Anson, his tone low and menacing. "A very short, painful existence."

His gaze snapped up to meet the Russian's. "Was that a threat?"

"Of course not, my friend." Nikolai's smile lasted the length of one heartbeat. "It was a promise." He turned and strode down the corridor. "*Dobroy nochi.*"

Goodnight the Russian bids after issuing a death threat. How could Nikolai be so cavalier with such things? Certainly, he could not be serious. And yet, Anson knew of Nikolai's reputation firsthand. His formative years spent in the military as a royal guard followed by his recruitment into one of the most secretive organizations on the continent. Such experience perfected his attention to detail and made him dangerous.

He sighed. Nikolai did not require a notebook. His memory served him better than a written log, as though it captured things in such perfect, photographic clarity, he need not rely on anything else. A curse, Nikolai once confessed.

A burst of frustration coursed through him. He pushed away thoughts of his missing notebook and Nikolai's threats before entering the room. Doctor Archer knelt on the floor examining Matilda's foot.

"Yes, my dear, it seems you have a laceration." He wrapped her foot with a fresh piece of linen from his medical bag. "But I would not worry. It looks clean and well-tended. I see no need for stitches." He tied the bandage securely. "But I would not put much weight on it for a week or two at least. That should give it ample time to heal properly."

"Thank you, doctor. I will be sure to follow your instructions." Matilda rewarded him with a smile.

He placed the remaining items back in his bag and rose to his feet. "You did a fine job tending to the wound, Major Montgomery." He fixed his glasses on the bridge of his nose. "Now, if you both will excuse me, I must see to my own supper."

Anson stepped aside and muttered his thanks as Doctor Archer took his leave. He closed the door behind him. Once they were alone, he fixed his gaze upon Matilda. He felt like a horse's ass.

"Can I get you anything?"

"Yes." Matilda's green eyes bore into his. "You can leave."

"Matilda." Her lashes fluttered at the sound of her name on his lips. "You must allow me to help you."

She rose and hobbled the short distance between them, careful not to put any pressure on her foot. "Will it ease your conscience?" Anger flashed in her eyes. "Will you just abandon me again once your guilt has been absolved?" She jabbed a finger in his chest. "I do not want your help, Major Montgomery."

He stared at her. A woman ripe with righteous indignation crowned in auburn curls. Her lips parted; her cheeks flushed with a delicate rosy hue.

Desire twisted in his gut like a flame dancing in darkness. Defeat surrounded him, constricting tighter and tighter with every breath. He closed his eyes, bracing for her scathing words or the sting of her palm across his cheek. "Then what do you want from me?"

Chapter Seventeen

Her heart thundered in her chest. Matilda gazed into the face of her tormentor. His soulful eyes hidden, and soft lips parted. The murmured question lingered between them. She studied his face. The silver hair at his temple glinted in the soft light. The shadow of a beard highlighted the strength of his jaw.

She flattened her palm against his chest and gathered the fabric of his waistcoat in her fist.

Anson's eyes flew open. A storm raged in their depths, dark and fathomless as the open sea at midnight.

Matilda pulled herself onto the tips of her toes. Pain shot through her foot, but she pushed it away and swayed. He caught her waist, forcing the space between them into nothingness. His heat radiated when she brought her lips closer.

"A kiss." She pressed her mouth against his. A ribbon of need unfurled inside her, creating a tangle of confusion and heat and desperation. She moaned when his grip tightened and he gathered her into his arms.

His mouth parted, and she darted her tongue across his lower lip, tasting him. The sharp bite of whisky mixed with the heady flavor that most surely belonged to him alone drew her into a haze. She slipped her hands over his shoulders and encircled her arms around his neck, pressing her body fully against his.

He plundered her mouth, and she allowed him entrance without hesitation. He sat down on the bed and set her in his lap. The kiss broke, and her delirious gaze found his. She threaded her fingers through his hair and rubbed her cheek against his. The stubble created a delicious friction against her smooth skin.

He stilled beneath her touch, but those warm hands remained firmly clasped around her waist.

"I love you, Anson." Matilda peppered the corner of his mouth with soft gentle kisses. "I have always loved you."

He closed his eyes and captured her mouth in a bruising kiss. It stole her breath. She fisted her hands in his hair. Seduction be damned. This was a siege.

As if freed from a spell, he slid his hands up her sides and buried them in her hair. She basked in her moment of triumph.

"Sweet Matilda." He roamed his hands along her spine. "You cannot know the torment I have suffered. What sweet torture." He met her gaze, desire and agony warring in his expression. Anson brushed a lock of hair from her face and cupped her jaw in his hand.

She nestled closer and purred with contentment. "Would you send me away now that you have tasted how sweet our love can be?"

Anson shook his head. "At this moment, you belong to me. Every part of you. From those lovely auburn curls—" he wrapped the errant curl around his finger "—to this irreverent mouth." His finger traced over her lips. "Heaven help me."

Matilda's soul took flight at his words. She kissed him again and fed her passion without fear of rejection.

He replied in kind. She twisted in his lap until she straddled him on the bed, hiking her skirt in bunches around her waist to better enjoy the press of his body beneath her own.

Anson gripped her arms and broke the kiss. She frowned at him.

"Matilda, stop." He soothed her disappointment with a kiss on the forehead. "I refuse to seduce you on a train in the mountains."

Matilda pouted. But that was exactly what she desired. All those years she pined for him and never knew precisely what she wanted. It now lay before her like a banquet feast. Matilda wallowed in frustration at his reluctance, crossing her arms while her mood soured.

He slid her from his lap to the bed and stood before facing her. His gaze softened. "Do not look at me in such a manner." He raked his hand through his hair. "Soon we shall be in Vienna.

I believe we both can refrain until then."

Joy blossomed where disappointment had taken root. "I can stay in Vienna?"

"Until your father arrives." Anson nodded. "Then we shall discuss it further."

Although it was not the affirmation she desired, Matilda grasped the opportunity he presented. She jumped up, uninhibited by her injury, and wrapped her arms around Anson. "Thank you." She nestled against his chest memorizing his scent and the warmth of his embrace.

"I just hope he does not kill me for absconding with his only daughter." His sigh ruffled her hair.

In all her life, Matilda could not remember a moment of such pure joy and perfection. She finally convinced him. Major Anson Montgomery was hers.

After a few moments, he pulled away. "That is quite enough excitement for one evening." He cleared his throat and opened the door. "I want you to lock this door and sleep. I shall come for you in the morning. We will arrive in Salzburg early."

"One last kiss?" She reached out her hand.

He shook his head. "Goodnight, Matilda."

"Goodnight, Anson."

He closed the door behind him.

Matilda collapsed on the bed in delirium. Could it really have been so simple? Kiss him first. *Who would have thought?*

Anson conceded defeat after a long night of tossing in his narrow bed and retreated to the lounge car as dawn broke over the alps. He ordered coffee and some toast to settle his stomach. Agitation roiled through him over events of the night before.

Why in the blazes of hell did he kiss her? He raked his hand over his face and growled under his breath. He vowed not to let desire cloud his judgement. Yet one soft, silken taste of her lips broke his restraint like an overflowing dam splitting its well-crafted bonds.

It could not happen again. His sweet and passionate words were lies. As much as he craved her companionship and her company in his bed, he could not in good conscience follow through with it. The veil of darkness and temptation drew the words from his lips in a windswept, passionate moment. One he did not regret stealing. Still, his conscience burned at the thought of revealing the truth. She would hate him for it most certainly.

The waiter placed a small tray on the table beside him.

Anson sipped the hot beverage. The warm, soothing scent surrounded him while he savored the bitter jolt on his tongue.

He had no choice. After one kiss, he realized only too acutely how much she affected him. Hopefully his telegram would reach Jacob quickly so he could retrieve his daughter post haste. Anson would hold his bargain to keep her safe, but the thought of having her in his home for a week made his blood heat. The fortitude it took to refrain from laying claim to her the night before physically pained him. His vague responses mollified her in the moment. But how long could he continue to deny the desire simmering between them?

Anson inhaled deeply and took another drink. Perhaps he could pay Mrs. Jennings double to watch her while he found temporary lodging elsewhere. At this point, he knew better than to allow even a moment for temptation to seize him by the cock and lead them both into ruination.

The compartment door opened and Dr. Archer entered the lounge. He nodded in acknowledgement.

"Good morning, Major Montgomery." Dr. Archer glanced around the otherwise empty train car. "Where is the lovely Mrs. Hudson this morning?"

"She is still abed." Anson forced himself not to think of the fact that he would still be with her in bed had he relented to his baser instincts. He shut the tantalizing thought from his mind. "Please, join me."

"I do hope she is quite revived today." The doctor sat in the chair opposite Anson and placed his book in his lap. "Such an injury is not detrimental, but it can be painful while it heals." The doctor adjusted his glasses and tapped his fingers on the cover of his well-worn book. "I will be disembarking in Salzburg. Will you and Mrs. Hudson as well?"

"Unfortunately, no. We will continue on to Vienna."

The doctor nodded with understanding. "I see. It is a shame. Salzburg is quite lovely this time of year." He chuckled. "Well, any time of year, really. Aside from my hometown and Paris, I believe it is the most beautiful city on the continent."

"I cannot argue with you on that point." Anson remembered the home he abandoned so long ago. London would always hold a piece of his heart, even if he could never again experience her splendor. He cleared his throat. "What brings you to Salzburg, doctor?"

Doctor Archer and Anson enjoyed a lengthy conversation, mostly on behalf of the doctor who gave a detailed account of his research and the convention he planned to attend in Vienna the following month. It proved diverting, at least well enough as to purge the soul-twisting conundrum of Matilda from his mind.

An hour later, the conductor entered the car and announced the imminent arrival at Salzburg station. The doctor took his leave, and Anson returned to his compartment. He paused outside of Matilda's room. Silence. She must still be asleep.

He pulled his watch from his pocket. Seven thirty-two. In his compartment, he gathered his greatcoat and hat.

The whistle signaled their arrival at the station. The floor swayed beneath him as the brakes engaged, slowing the train. He lifted the curtain and watched the platform come into view. According to the schedule, he had thirty minutes before the train departed for Vienna.

He pulled on his coat and hat, then stepped out into the corridor. He pushed past Matilda's room and out into the winter air.

Curls of steam and smoke wove around the patrons and porters on the platform. The icy bite of the November air sank into his exposed skin. He pulled the coat closed at his throat before proceeding toward the warm glow of the station. The sooner he sent the telegram, the quicker he could ensure Matilda's reunion with her parents.

A warm cocoon enveloped him as he entered the station. He located the telegraph office beside the ticket window.

The attendant glanced up from his papers. "May I help you, sir?"

"I wish to send a message straightaway." Anson deposited a few coins on the counter.

The attendant nodded and drew out his pen and pad. "Go ahead, sir."

"Matilda is safe. Come to Vienna immediately. Reply to my home address. Montgomery." Anson gave the address of their Paris residence and Jacob's full name. "Please send it as soon as possible."

"I shall send it right away, sir. Anything else?"

"No, thank you." Anson exhaled a deep breath as the clerk turned to send the telegram. He waited until the man returned with confirmation the message had been sent and received at the next station.

Anson returned to the cold, steam laden platform. The magnificent engine stood stark against the snow-covered buildings and the mountain peaks rising in the distance. He admired the sleek lines enhanced with blue and gold paint. The train's name, Alpine Express, emblazoned upon the side of the coal car behind the engineer housing on the massive engine. Smoke and steam billowed from the stack.

His gaze followed the porters as they led the final guests and their luggage aboard. The conductor paced the length of the train. *Signora* Castellan's two minions lingered toward the rear of the train on the platform, cigarettes in hand.

As he approached, they turned their attention toward him. Ever since he realized their connection to *Signora* Castellan, he could not dismiss the suspicion they had something to do with his missing journal and the state of his compartment. He would pay a call on the widow once he returned to Vienna.

"All aboard!" The conductor's voice echoed across the platform. "Final call for the Alpine Express to Vienna." His shrill whistle pierced the early morning chill.

The two men flicked their cigarettes to the ground and

boarded the train.

With a grunt, Anson stepped up onto the carriage and into the lounge. Inside, he braced himself against the wall as the train whistle blew and the mechanical beast lurched into motion. Once he found steady footing, he removed his coat and hat. He wove through the lounge and entered the sleeping car preceding his own.

Nikolai stepped through the door. "Good morning, my friend. Care to join me?"

Anson shook his head. "I must check on Matilda."

The Russian rested his hand on his shoulder. "She is in Gertrude's compartment."

"Perhaps I should check—" His voice trailed off at the smirk on Nikolai's lips.

"She is safe. Believe me." Nikolai clapped his hand on his back. Anson winced at the force of the blow. "Come, you can tell me all about your conquest while we break our fast."

Anson bit back a retort as they retraced his steps back through the lounge car and entered the dining car. Once they sat, he frowned at Nikolai's curious gaze.

"What happened last evening?"

"A gentleman would never ask such a question." Anson stifled his irritation.

"I have never claimed to be a gentleman, major, and you know that. We have shared many tales. I remember you once told me about a lewd show you attended in Istanbul. What are a few intimate details among friends?"

"Nothing happened." Anson fought to keep an impassive expression while he met the Russian's intense gaze.

"Nothing?" He looked almost disappointed. "Not even a kiss."

The memory of her soft lips, questing tongue, and sweet taste surged to the surface. As long as he lived, he would never forget how perfectly she fit against his body or her desperate mewling sounds when kissed her throat. He groaned.

Nikolai grinned. "She took my advice then."

Anger sliced through the pleasurable memory. "Advice?"

He leaned across the table. "What the hell are you talking about? What did you tell her to do?"

"Nothing as vulgar as you would believe. I merely advised her to take the first step, since you seemed so adamant to play the gentleman."

Fury surged through Anson. "How could you do such a thing? She is only a child."

Nikolai's expression sharpened, and the humor dissolved instantly. "She is no child, Anson. In case you have not yet realized it, she loves you." He folded his arms across his chest. "You are a fool if you cannot realize what a valuable treasure you have before you waiting to be claimed."

"I have nothing to offer her. No title, no land, no wealth, no security. I can never return to England. She deserves someone in their prime with the world at his feet." Anson glanced out the window, unable to meet Nikolai's intrusive gaze.

"If you truly believe that, then I pity you. You will regret this." Nikolai tapped the table with his index finger to emphasize his words. "Believe me."

"At this moment, the only thing I regret is not turning you into the Royal guards when I had the chance," Anson snapped, irritation and anger churning inside him.

Nikolai's countenance darkened. "Do not threaten me. We both share the blame for that night."

"And I paid my penance for it." Anson stood abruptly. "You hid. Coward." Without a backward glance, he stormed from the dining car.

History and friendship be damned. The Russian finally pushed him to the point of combustion. This explosive confrontation confirmed Anson's worst fear. Nikolai Voronia could not be trusted.

CHAPTER EIGHTEEN

On the Alpine Express
November 17, 1899

Matilda bolted upright, gripping the side of the bed. The train's shrill whistle made her heart constrict. She pressed her hand to her chest and exhaled deeply to calm herself. One moment Anson held her in a loving embrace deep in a blissful dream, the next it lay shattered by reality. How rude.

She smiled. Soon, they would be in Vienna, and she would no longer have to dream about such a moment. He would be hers. Completely.

Matilda stood. The train did not sway beneath her feet. She dashed for the curtain and glanced out the window. A snow-covered station stood beyond the glass, the name Salzburg painted in gold and red letters above the archway. Steam mingled with the cold creating a dense fog on the platform and several dark figures shuffled through the haze. She strained to see details beyond the station, but to no avail. How long had they been stopped? She longed to catch a glimpse of the city, however fleeting.

Quickly, she pulled on her black woolen gown and tied her hair in a precarious bun at her nape. She fastened the black net over it and pinned it into place. With a nod of satisfaction in the mirror behind the door, she peered into the hallway.

Why did Anson not wake her? She caught a glimpse of a retreating form as she rounded the corner and disappeared through the connecting door leading to her sleeping car.

Matilda closed her compartment and hurried after her friend, excitement coursing through her. She longed to tell Gertrude what happened between her and Anson. Careful of her injured foot, she proceeded down the corridor and into the next car. Which compartment belonged to Gertrude? Perhaps she should wait until later in the lounge car.

Matilda counted three sleeping compartments. This car contained the same as her own. If Nikolai and Gertrude were accompanying the countess, then all three compartments must belong to them. She shrugged. A one in three chance of finding Gertrude seemed fine odds. She selected the middle compartment and knocked.

"Who is it?"

"It is Matilda."

The door swung open. Gertrude wore the same dirndl as the previous day. Her vibrant blue eyes seemed muted to a pale grey in the dim morning light.

"*Guten Morgen.*" Matilda practically bounced on her toes.

"*Guten Morgen, liebing.*" Gertrude opened door wider and gestured for Matilda to enter. "Please come in. I trust you slept well."

Matilda chuckled. "I slept so well, I nearly missed Salzburg completely."

Gertrude nodded. "We will only be here for short while. By nightfall we shall be in Vienna."

"I wish I could have seen the city. I hear Salzburg is beautiful."

"It is." Gertrude opened the curtains, revealing the platform and the station beyond. "Perhaps one day you can return and enjoy the delights this region has to offer."

"Perhaps." Matilda pressed her cheek against the glass as she scanned the scene outside. The steam dissipated enough to reveal the passengers standing upon the platform. She recognized the two men who were traveling together and the conductor who paced the length of the train.

Tall and broad against the shadowed station, Anson stepped forward, his gaze turned toward the fore of the train. Even from this distance, she recognized his strong profile.

"I see the major decided to stretch his legs a bit." Gertrude followed Matilda's attention.

"Mmmhmm." The sight of him in his greatcoat and hat brought the memory of their first meeting flashing through her mind. She opened the door, and he stood on the doorstep in the exact manner. Tall, handsome, imposing, and confident. When he smiled at her, she knew, even at the young age, she would love him forever.

The conductors whistle echoed outside. Anson quickened his pace, as did the other two men. She followed him with her gaze until he disappeared from view. Matilda sighed.

"*Liebling*, have you come to an understanding with the handsome major? Or is he still adamant in his refusal?"

The whistle interjected twice before falling silent, and the train lurched into motion. Both women swayed, bracing their hands on the wall. Once they found their footing, Matilda dropped her hand and met her friend's gaze.

"I believe we have. I took your and Mr. Voronia's advice."

Gertrude's eyes widened and her mouth opened in surprise. "Nikolai gave you advice?"

"Well, yes, in a way."

"What did he suggest?" Gertrude blinked as though stunned by this revelation.

"He suggested I tell Anson of my love. I told him I did as much and been rebuffed, thrice. Then he observed that sometimes actions are much better than words."

A strong shade of scarlet stained Gertrude's pale skin. "*Och, mein Gott in Himmel.*" Gertrude sat on her bed and pressed her hand to her mouth.

Matilda stared. It was not advice as much as an observation.

"He was not wrong, *liebling.*" Gertrude dropped her hand and choked laughter bubbled from her parted lips. "But Nikolai knows nothing of a woman's heart."

"Well, you did tell me to kiss him first. Is that not similar in a way?"

"I suppose that is true." Gertrude's eyes lit with curiosity. "So, you took my advice?"

"Yes." She pressed her fingertips to her lips, remembering the feel of his mouth against hers.

Gertrude smiled. "I have half a mind to follow your lead."

"Perhaps you should."

Gertrude's smile faded into a wistful smirk. "I have no intention of being bound to any man, and Nikolai Voronia is full of dark secrets and sweet lies." Her gaze hardened. She pursed her lips and scowled at the passing scenery before shaking her head. When she met Matilda's gaze, her joy returned.

A great pounding commenced on the wall behind Gertrude. Matilda jumped, startled. She glanced at Gertrude in question. "What was that?"

"Oh, that would be the countess. I should fetch her breakfast." She opened the suitcase on the bed and removed an apron.

"I have not seen her during the trip." Matilda realized with a jolt of concern. "Does she not feel well?"

"The countess dislikes traveling, although she does it quite frequently. I believe it is the novelty of changing cities that fortifies her for the trip itself." Gertrude tied on the apron. "She dislikes eating in public, so I bring meals to her compartment."

"Would you like some help?"

Another series of blows shook the wall. Matilda's eyes widened.

A nervous chuckle escaped Gertrude. "No, thank you. I must go. Shall we meet for afternoon tea?"

"That sounds lovely."

"I shall see you then." Gertrude hurried from the room.

Matilda heard the neighboring door open and the sound of two women conversing through the open door. Gertrude forgot to replace her luggage. She intended to close the suitcase and put it on the shelf when she noticed a leather journal peeking from beneath a cream-colored blouse. She pushed the garment aside and smiled.

"She found her journal." Matilda brushed her fingers over the cover and traced the embossed gold letters on the bottom corner. She replaced the blouse and closed the suitcase.

After she left Gertrude's compartment, Matilda walked along the corridor, skimming her fingers along the mahogany sideboard until she reached the adjoining car. It seemed all her dreams were coming to fruition.

Matilda paused outside Anson's room. Was he inside? Perhaps he was in the dining car. She would check there first. She ignored the pressure in her foot and wandered in the direction of a hearty breakfast and a hot cup of tea. Only Anson's presence could make her joy complete.

By evening, Matilda would be in his home and, hopefully, in his bed.

CHAPTER NINETEEN

When the train arrived in Vienna, Matilda could barely contain her excitement. She winced as she stepped onto the platform. Damn and blast her foot for ruining her first real adventure. She longed to race ahead of Anson and drink in the city.

The sun set before they reached the station, cloaking the surrounding city in darkness. But the glow of the lamps illuminated the platform and the sign emblazoned on the archway. *Weiner Banhof.* Vienna Station.

She vibrated with excitement. Matilda pulled her coat a bit tighter around her throat to protect it from the alpine chill. Her breath curled in small wisps in the cold air.

Anson directed the porter to have their baggage delivered to his home. He turned, his face half-obscured by the tilt of his hat.

"Shall we?" He proffered his arm.

Matilda wrapped her gloved hand around it, thankful for his physical support. It seemed she may have overdone it wandering the train that morning. Her foot protested with a throbbing ache. She hobbled forward, determined to enjoy this new adventure.

"Your foot pains you."

"Just a bit." She dismissed it with a laugh. Pain stabbed through her with every impact. She hissed in a breath when they stepped onto the uneven cobbled street.

"Wait here." Anson approached one of the waiting cabs and spoke with the driver. Within moments, they rode into the Vienna night.

Matilda leaned out of the carriage window in a vain attempt to soak in every possible detail of the city. It resembled London and Paris in some respects, but Vienna showcased her own unique character through the architecture.

The lamps along the river reflected in the water. A lovely walking path lay along the street designated only for pedestrians. The moonlight shone brilliant in the sky overhead.

Their carriage ambled up the street until it came to a long row of townhomes nestled just across the street from the river and rolled to a stop in front of them. Matilda admired the brick and stone as well as the delicate iron railing on either side of the steps leading to the front doors. This would be her home? Joy effused her.

Anson climbed from the carriage, paid the driver, and offered his hand to Matilda. She took it, aware of the pain in her foot as she put pressure on it once more.

He swept her into his arms. She grasped his greatcoat at the unexpected movement. Their faces hovered close. His breath mingled with hers in the frosty night air. Even in the dim streetlight, Matilda recognized the hunger in his eyes. Her fingers tightened on the wool, and she licked her lips.

The carriage rattled away, leaving them in blissful solitude.

His gaze shuttered before he strode up the stairs and set her upon the top step. He knocked three times on the sturdy door.

They waited barely a moment when the door swung open.

"Well, my heavens, come in, come in." A short, curvy woman stepped to the side and allowed them admittance into the house. "Welcome home, major."

"Thank you, Mrs. Jennings." He ushered Matilda inside the door.

The simple woodwork and muted shades of blue and gray created a homey feeling inside the hallway. A staircase rose to a second floor at the rear, and a doorway lay on either side of them.

"This is Miss Hudson. She will be staying with us for a short while." Anson gestured to her. "If you would not mind preparing the second bedroom, please."

Matilda blinked. Second bedroom. Staying for a short while. He quelled her questioning look with a single shake of his head. She bit back a frown.

"Of course, major." Mrs. Jennings turned her attention to

Matilda. "You must be exhausted from your journey, my dear. I shall draw you a nice hot bath and have some supper prepared."

"That sounds wonderful." Matilda's spirits lifted once more.

"Follow Mrs. Jennings. She will get you anything you require." His weak smile faltered. "I have some business to attend."

Mrs. Jennings whisked her down the hall and up to the second floor. Her heart ached even more than her foot at the thought of being separated from Anson. She frowned and followed the housekeeper.

Anson remained distant all day. What little time they spent together, he kept his responses stilted and brusque. She attributed his attitude to a lack of sleep. Lord knows, she struggled to fall asleep the night before. After their kiss, she laid awake for hours imagining what pleasures awaited her in Vienna.

Mrs. Jennings led her into a small bedroom. The deep blue curtains matched the coverlet on the four-poster bed opposite a matching wardrobe. A light blue trunk decorated with flowers and birds sat under the window. The bath lay in the adjoining room. She admired the space with delight while Mrs. Jennings drew water into the beautiful tub.

"I shall let you bathe in peace. Let me fetch you a few items from my chamber. Heaven knows we have never hosted a lady in residence. I am sure you will not mind using mine until your luggage arrives." The housekeeper's warm smile made her feel welcome. "Be back in a moment."

"Thank you."

Mrs. Jennings slipped from the room.

Matilda walked into the bathroom. Warm steam filled the room. She sighed in appreciation even though her foot protested when she removed her shoes.

After Mrs. Jennings returned and retreated once more, Matilda undressed and sank into the luxurious, steaming waters. Her foot ceased its torturous demands.

With an appreciative moan, she relaxed and the rose-scented water washed her concern away.

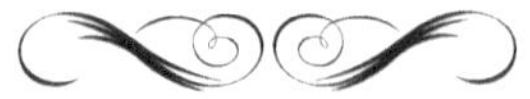

Anson's gaze followed Matilda as she climbed the stairs. Once she disappeared from view, he exhaled a sharp breath. His conscience rallied against him. He shook his head and retreated into his study.

The scent of leather and woodsmoke enveloped him. He relaxed the moment he stepped into the familiar space. The room lay neat and tidy, as he left it, free of dust thanks to the careful attention of the maid and Mrs. Jennings. His attention fell to the pile of letters lying on his desk.

Anson flicked through the pile and noted the return address on the top three before pushing them aside. A telegram. He plucked the paper from the pile and opened it.

On my way to Vienna. Keep Matilda safe. Do nothing you will regret. – Jacob. November 15, 1899

He blinked and read the telegram three times. Upon the last reading, Anson paused, his thumb under the date.

How could this be possible? He only sent the telegram that morning. He left Paris on November fifteenth. Two days ago. His heart jolted into a rhythmic tattoo. Somehow Jacob knew exactly where his daughter had gone, and the finger of blame pointed squarely at himself. He closed his eyes and cursed, tossing the telegram onto his desk. It fluttered to the floor behind it instead.

"Son of a bitch." Anson stalked across the room and poured two fingers of scotch into a crystal glass. He tossed the liquid down his throat. The burn nearly made him choke. He poured another and chased the first. This time it went down smooth, comforting him with the promise of blissful abandon.

He raked his hand through his hair. How could Jacob possibly know Matilda was with him? *Do nothing you will regret.* What the hell was he trying to say? Guilt plagued his conscience from the moment he found Matilda on that train. Her profession of love twisted a knife in his gut. He warred with his better judgement during the entire journey. How could he explain the extent of his torment to his best friend? Jacob's duty as a father far superseded their friendship.

At some point, Anson would face Jacob's wrath. This was a certainty. He hoped to mollify it by explaining her desire for adventure drove her to act in such a rash manner. Jacob knew of their correspondence. There had never been anything untoward in all those years. Never the slightest hint of impropriety or scandal. Until this.

The telegram confirmed his worst possible fear. Jacob knew the truth. He somehow discovered Matilda's longstanding infatuation with him and assumed Anson stole her away. Jacob believed the worst of him. A man unable to curb his own desires, unable to protect those placed in his care. Shame flickered through him, ignited by the misery and the sweet siren call of the liquor. He set the glass down in irritation.

His dearest friend would reclaim what Anson had taken and end their longstanding friendship. No amount of penance could repair such a wound.

Absorbed in his thoughts, Anson dismissed the distant sound of knocking. When it persisted, he grunted and mumbled beneath his breath praying it was not Jacob. Not yet.

Anson wrenched the door open and glared at the intrusion upon his tumultuous solitude.

Signora Castellan stood upon the stoop wrapped in fur and velvet. Diamonds glittered in her ears reflecting the light from inside his home.

"What business could you possibly have here, *signora?*" Irritation filled him. He fully intended to call upon her at some point and discuss the presence of her men on the train. But at that moment, her lackeys were the furthest thing from his mind. "I warn you. I have little patience this evening."

"I am not surprised." *Signora* Castellan pushed past him and stepped into the hallway. She turned in a circle as if searching for something, her dark eyes sparkling, and her red lips curved into a devilish smile. "Well, where is she?"

Anson closed the door with an irritated grunt. "I assume your accomplices informed you of my return."

"Of course." She waved a hand and glanced around again. "They also told me of your lovely, young companion."

He should have tossed the two men out in the snow when he had the chance. He returned to his study, uncaring whether she followed or not. He poured two glasses of scotch and offered one to his uninvited guest.

She draped her fur coat on the chair near the fire. Her emerald green velvet gown and the cluster of diamonds at her throat drew a stark contrast against his modest home.

"*Grazie*." She held the glass up to the light and swirled the liquor. "Well?"

"Tell me why your henchmen were that train." Anson sipped the drink, still feeling the effects from the last two glasses he imbibed.

She drank. The motion accentuated the graceful curve of her jaw and the slim line of her neck. He wanted to break it. Infuriating woman.

"They retrieved some items I procured from a specialty shop in Paris." She shrugged her shoulder. Her gaze leveled with his, unwavering.

"I caught them ransacking the luggage car." He set his drink aside and folded his arms across his chest. "Suspicious behavior to say the least."

Signora Castellan pursed her lips and tapped her fingernail against the crystal glass clutched in her right hand. "They misplaced an irreplaceable item. They did not realize it until the train was half way to Vienna. *Stupido*." She spat the last word under her breath with vehemence.

"You expect me to believe their presence on that train was purely coincidental?" He searched her expression for a fault or slip, something proving her lies.

"Of course, it was." She raised a delicate brow. "When they returned and told me of your presence on the train, complete with a young redheaded companion, well, I could hardly wait to see her for myself." She finished the scotch and set the glass aside. "This mythical creature who has captured the attention of the handsome, and elusive, Major Montgomery."

"Whom I travel with is of no concern to you." Anson remained impassive, but her goading only infuriated him more.

"Since you mention traveling companions, I find it curious that our Russian friend also traveled on the same train." *Signora* Castellan sidled up to him, her lashes brushing against the pale skin of her cheek before she met his gaze. "One would think you choose your friends more carefully, Major."

Anson took a deep breath. He walked away, putting as much distance as possible between them. "We were not traveling together. Nikolai escorted the Countess von Breunner and her traveling companion back to Vienna."

Her brow arched. "Interesting."

"What?"

"I have it on the highest authority that Countess von Breunner did not return on the Alpine Express with Nikolai and her companion." She rested her finger against her lower lip and tapped it. "The countess is in Paris as we speak, attending a celebratory gala."

A trickle of fear penetrated his defenses. If she was correct, then Anson had been taken for a fool. What farce had Nikolai and Fräulein Bleul been playing? He schooled his features, feigning disinterest. "What should it matter to me?"

"I warned you once before, *bello*." *Signora* Castellan stepped close and rested her hand on his chest. "He is Okhrana. You cannot trust him."

"But I can trust you?"

"I only wish to offer my—" she licked her lips "—support. Should you find yourself in need of a friend."

Anson gripped her wrists and removed her hands from his person. "You should leave."

Signora Castellan pouted before retrieving her coat from the chair. "If you change your mind—" she slipped the luxurious garment onto her body "—you know where to find me."

He followed her to the door and closed it firmly behind her. The burst of cold air quelled the heat rising inside him. How could he have been so foolish? Had he been so blind, so distracted by Matilda's presence, he missed every sign of Nikolai's deception? He returned to his study and paced.

The trip replayed in his mind. Every conversation. Every encounter. All of it had been focused on him and Matilda. Damn it. He never saw the countess aboard the Alpine Express because she was never on the train.

Anson tripped over his feet as he rushed into the hallway. He pulled on his great coat and hat as he stepped out into the frosty evening. The door slammed behind him. He glanced up at the building he called home for the last five years.

Matilda would be safe. Safer than if he were inside with her. He would return soon.

Anson strode into the night, desperate to wring the truth from the man who once saved his life and earned him the censure of his homeland. Nikolai owed him that much.

CHAPTER TWENTY

Matilda donned a plush robe over her warm nightgown. She stepped from her bed chamber into the hall. Curiosity consumed her. Anson's voice echoed up the stairs followed by a woman's reply. Mrs. Jennings? She lifted the hem of her nightgown and crept down the staircase, aware of the pounding of her own heart.

She reached the landing and slid along the wall, keeping to the shadows as she approached the room near the front entrance. The firelight flickered against the open door. Two distinct voices sounded from within. The Anson's enchanting timbre countered by the lovely accented cadence of a woman.

Grazie. Italian? A nagging uncertainty pricked at her mind. Matilda peeked around the corner, careful to remain hidden.

Their voices remained low but distinct. Who were they talking about? Matilda's breath caught as she strained to follow their conversation. Her heart raced. She smoothed her palms on the robe.

"This mythical creature who has captured the attention of the handsome, and elusive, Major Montgomery."

The conversation shifted quickly. Were they speaking of Nikolai? Did this woman know him as well? Were they all acquaintances? Matilda attempted to catch a glimpse of the woman, but she stood too far into the room. Anson's strong profile stood stark in her vision, amplified by the firelight. Murderous. Vengeful. Seeing Anson in such a state both terrified and aroused her.

"I have it on the highest authority that Countess von Breunner did not return on the Alpine Express with Nikolai and her companion." The woman paused, her tone filled with satisfaction at delivering the message. "The countess is in Paris as we speak, attending a celebratory gala."

Matilda frowned. But she heard the countess in the adjoining compartment when she visited with Gertrude that morning.

"He is Okhrana. You cannot trust him." The words drifted through the doorway, leaving Matilda confused.

What is Okhrana? Who were they talking about? Before she could put any more thought into the exchange, Matilda glimpsed the woman in Anson's company. She looked regal, her svelte figure swathed in yards of green velvet and her throat encased with gemstones glinting in the firelight. Dark hair curled in large ringlets pinned upon her head. Sophisticated. Powerful. Mature. Disappointment coursed through Matilda. She was none of those things.

Unable to watch, Matilda pressed her back against the wall. Her heart threatened to break. Who was this woman?

"If you change your mind, you know where to find me." The woman's voice came closer.

Matilda gasped. They were coming into the hall. As quick as her foot allowed, Matilda dashed across the hall and into a darkened room. She hid in the shadows, fearful they spotted her.

After a moment, the front door closed with a loud thud. Matilda peered out of the room and spied Anson's back as he retreated into his study.

Go to him. Her heart pleaded. But the uncertainty of what she just witnessed left her paralyzed. She waited in the dark room and pressed her hand to her chest. *Go to him.* After a few moments, Matilda's courage fortified. She stepped from the hall, only to see the front door slam closed.

A gust of cold enveloped her. She wrapped her arms around herself and hobbled into the study. He was gone.

Matilda frowned. Where did he go? After the woman? Her heart sank into the pit of her stomach. What did she expect?

With a sigh, Matilda trailed her fingers across his large carved desk. She circled around it and sat in his chair. It provided a perfect view of the tall bookcases and the large iron fireplace. Her gaze fell on the stack of mail piled on the silver tray.

She smoothed her hands across the desk drawer. Curious, she opened it, finding stationary, ink, wax seal, several sticks of wax, and a silver letter opener. She pushed it closed and reached for the drawer on the bottom. Inside, an ornate wooden box lay tucked beneath a stack of papers.

After gently setting the papers aside, Matilda lifted the box from its hiding place. The latch was unlocked. She licked her lips and pried the lid open. A gasp escaped her.

Her letters. She thumbed through each letter, filed by date, each penned in her hand. The first in her inexperienced, childish writing, but as she progressed deeper into the contents of the box, the penmanship grew more elegant, more familiar. Tears pricked at her eyes and pride filled her heart. He kept every letter.

The letters were faded and well-read. Her words were almost illegible. The tears fell freely. Did she really mean this much to him? He treasured her letters. In truth, she saved every one of his, but was that not the actions of a woman in love?

With care, Matilda replaced the letters in the box and returned it to the drawer. As she placed the papers back on top, her hand brushed leather. She withdrew a leather journal and held it up to the light.

Familiar embossed initials lay on the dark leather jacket. Where had she seen such craftmanship before? She pushed the nagging thought aside and opened it. Within the pages, Matilda found dates, events, names, descriptions, and other minute details. The random notes of the entries piqued her interest.

"Lady Gorcey and her husband. On the rocks. Noted flirtation with Madame Traun, Piedmont Ball, Prague, 1894." Matilda read each entry under her breath and giggled at the simplistic descriptions while imagining the scenarios they documented.

Contented for the moment, Matilda curled up in the wingback chair beside the fire. She cradled the journal in her lap. Perhaps Anson's journal could enlighten her. As she read, she heard his voice in her mind. His jaded, but organized, commentary on the social classes in which he moved engrossed her.

What delightful secrets would she uncover?

The five-story building loomed in the shadowed moonlight. Anson's breath came in agitated puffs from the exertion of making his way through the city on foot in addition to the fury boiling inside him. During their journey, Nikolai lied. He pretended to be something he most assuredly was not. Their friendship was a farce. Perhaps he should have heeded *Signora* Castellan's revelation of Nikolai's dark, secretive past years before.

Anson shook his head. No. He could not believe it, and yet the truth seemed undeniable. Nikolai had always been secretive, able to wield manipulation to an effective degree without attracting undue attention.

He ascended the stairs two at a time and entered the apartment building. Nikolai preferred to live beneath his means, even though he earned a handsome income for his service to the countess. He chose to live in a humble apartment just beyond his employer's reach.

He stalked up the stairs to the fifth floor. After a pause to catch his breath, Anson hammered his fist on the door tucked in the back of the building. Number twenty-five.

"Nikolai!" Anson continued his assault without thought of the neighboring tenants. "Open the damn door!" He pounded harder. Irritation swelled inside him. He grasped the handle and twisted it. Locked.

He had half a mind to kick it down. Anson raked his hand through his hair.

"What in the devil are you about?" A wizened voice came from the opposite side of the hallway. "Waking half the building with your ruckus."

"My apologies, sir." Anson spun around. His face burned. "I was merely concerned for my friend's welfare."

"Well, I would be more concerned about the woman." The old man stepped into the dim lighting. His stooped figure and lined face belied his age, but his eyes sparkled with a youthful glow. "I heard them arguing through the wall. When I stepped out to tell them to quiet down, that man tossed her over his shoulder and carried her down the stairs. Her curses rattled the whole building."

Anson's brow furrowed. The woman must have been Gertrude. "When was this?"

"An hour past." He shook his head. "Youth is wasted on the young."

Anson grumbled. They could be anywhere. "Thank you, sir."

The old man waved a hand and disappeared back into his apartment.

In the short amount of time it took for Anson to make his way to the count's home, he mulled over the possibilities. He assumed Nikolai and Gertrude were partners in their deception. But it seemed there were deeper undercurrents to their relationship than Anson realized.

Only the count could confirm if *Signora* Castellan's words bore any truth. He pulled his watch from his waistcoat pocket. Nearly eleven. Would the count even be home? Anson cursed. It did not matter. He needed confirmation either way.

Illuminated windows scattered across the ghostly white façade of the distinctive Viennese marble building. Shadows moved inside the large window on the ground floor. He prayed the count would admit him into his home.

The guard outside the gate drew his weapon. "What business have you here?"

"Major Anson Montgomery, emissary to the British Ambassador. I wish to speak with Count von Breunner. It is a matter of great importance." Anson waited as the guard summoned someone from the house.

He tapped his finger against his leg while his gaze skimmed over the house. His mind spun a web of unanswered questions and impossibilities. How long had Nikolai abused their friendship?

The guard reappeared and unlocked the gate. He stepped

aside, watching Anson with suspicion.

Inside the house, the chill of the November air dissipated into a luxurious warmth. Anson removed his hat and spun it in his hands. Vibrant tapestries and gilded furniture lined the entranceway. A well-dressed butler led him into one of several rooms veering off in all directions.

Elegance and extravagance tied intricately into the whole aristocratic livelihood. No matter how much time Anson spent in such opulence, it never appealed to him. His gaze fell on the man with whom he needed to speak.

Count von Breunner turned, a snifter of brandy in his hand and a cigar tucked in between the portly fingers of the other. He tucked the cigar between his lips and inhaled deeply. Smoke curled around his face and entangled in his bushy white mustache.

"Major Montgomery. What could possibly be so urgent it could not wait until morning?"

"My lord, I apologize for disturbing you so late." Anson searched for the most delicate way to broach the topic and found they all lacked decorum. He threw caution into the flames and chose the direct approach. Propriety be damned. "Is Mr. Voronia still in your employment?"

The count puffed on his cigar before pulling it from his lips. He set it in the crystal ash tray on the mantle. "The Russian. Well, I certainly hope he is. Unless my wife decided she no longer desired her prized hound dogging her heels." No bitterness tainted his words, merely humor.

"You did not hire him?"

The count shook his head. "No. My wife returned from visiting family in St. Petersburg and brought him in tow." He shrugged. "She claimed he saved our son's life or some such nonsense and hired him to be her personal protector."

Anson nodded. He never heard how Nikolai came into the service of the countess, but then again, the Russian never offered personal details. Being in Nikolai's company encouraged the impression the most interesting topic was anything but himself.

"Do you know where Mr. Voronia is now, my lord?"

"Paris, I suppose. The countess is attending a gala this evening and will be returning on the Bavarian Express within the week. I can only assume he is guarding her as a fierce hound would his mistress. Why, what does this inquisition regard?"

The skin on Anson's neck prickled. "I wished to confirm the countess is safe. There have been rumors of those who wish harm upon members of the royal Russian family. It is my duty to relay information that could prevent such a catastrophe."

The count's gaze narrowed. "I have heard such rumors myself, but rest assured, she is well-protected."

"My lord." He bowed. "I am your humble servant."

With a sniff, the count turned away. "You are dismissed."

Anson did not need to be told a second time. He removed himself from the count's gaudy home and his overindulgent presence. The rotund, bewhiskered man apparently did not find Anson's presence or concerns worth noting. He never investigated the history of the man who protected his wife and children. Even if he did, he did not care one wit. It was beneath him to concern himself with such trivialities.

Out on the cold, dark street, Anson pulled his collar up and tucked his hands in his pockets. Nikolai could be anywhere in the city. Hell, he could be on a train out of the city. Damn it.

Anson kept a brisk pace as he returned home. The city streets wove like a maze in the dark, but he walked them enough times to know he could find his home blindfolded.

Home. The image that appeared in his mind was not a place. It was a person. *Matilda.* He despised leaving her alone when all he wanted was to spend what little time remained in her presence. Damn.

Hatred filled him. Nikolai lied. Perhaps he had a legitimate reason for leaving the countess in Paris and lying about her presence on the train. No one asked him to uncover the deception or stalk the man he once considered an ally and a friend. Anson's conscience refused to relinquish the burning desire to know the truth.

Was the entirety of their friendship a charade? A pang of disgust twisted in his gut. He owed Nikolai a debt. Such a bond should have been unbreakable, but it lay in ruins, infested with distrust and secrets.

He should let it go. Disappointment sank into his bones and exhaustion consumed him. Even though they parted with harsh words, Anson could not harbor lingering resentment toward Nikolai. He had been the only other person aside from Jacob who offered a semblance of friendship.

Anson glanced up at his home. Inside those walls, the only person in the world Anson truly wanted to protect waited. The only soul he wanted to claim. His heart ached at the rift it would cause between himself and Jacob.

He would always sacrifice his own happiness to protect her. Matilda embodied all that was pure and innocent in the world. He would be damned if he stole that from her. When Jacob arrived, he would do the right thing.

She deserved better.

CHAPTER TWENTY-ONE

A loud pounding echoed in the hallway. Matilda dropped the journal and jumped to her feet as the noise persisted. She limped, careful of her bandaged foot, to the door leading to the hall.

Mrs. Jennings appeared from the rear of the house bundled in a thick housecoat covering her ample curves. She glanced at Matilda with a hesitant smile before reaching the door. Another quick succession of resounding booms pummeled the wood.

"In all my days." Mrs. Jennings opened the door.

The moment she turned the handle, the door twisted from under her hand and swung open, forced from the outside. Mrs. Jennings jumped aside with a startled squeak.

From out of the cold Viennese night, her parents appeared. Her heart sank at the sight of them. They arrived more quickly than she imagined possible.

"Mama, Papa, what are you doing here?" Matilda stepped into the hallway.

"Matilda!" Her mother ran across the room and pulled her into a tight, desperate embrace. Her mother's warm tears smeared her cheeks along with peppered kisses.

Flustered, Mrs. Jennings closed the door behind the two unexpected guests. "I will leave you." She disappeared down the hall, wide-eyed at the reunion causing such a commotion.

Matilda broke free from her mother's hold. "How is this possible? Anson was only able to send you a message this morning."

Her mother turned to her father, wringing her hands.

"The letter." His low, dangerous tone terrified her. Her father's gaze raked over her as if confirming she possessed all of her faculties and appendages. His handsome, familiar face, often graced with an easy smile, lay vacant of all humor. Lines etched across his forehead and dark circles beneath his eyes emphasized his age. He scowled at her. In all of her life, Matilda witnessed her father's anger only a handful of times, and it had never been directed at her. Until now.

Shame flooded her under his scrutiny and his words. "What letter?" Her response sounded weak. She knew exactly which letter. The one she found missing when she boarded the train in Paris.

"This one." Her father pulled a neatly folded, well-read letter from the inside pocket of his jacket and held it between two fingers.

Even from this distance, she could read her name on the outside of the parchment. Her gaze dropped to her feet. She studied the white bandage wrapped around her foot, unable to meet her parents' eyes. How could she have been so careless with the one item which damned both her and Anson?

Several tense moments passed. The grandfather clock ticked on the mantle in Anson's study. The soft noise punctuated her thundering heartbeat.

"Where is he?" Her father's tone cut through the silence like a honed blade.

"He left, just before you arrived." Matilda dared a glance at her mother, who seemed torn between maintaining her silence and reaching for her. Her eyes glittered with unshed tears.

Her father shook his head and stalked toward the study behind Matilda. She stepped out of the way. He poured himself a tall glass of scotch from the decanter sitting by the window.

Matilda took her mother's hand and followed him into the room. Her mother smoothed her fingers across her knuckles in a soothing motion. At least she showed a small measure of compassion. Matilda glanced at her mother, pleading with her eyes what she dare not speak until she could be sure of her father's tempered rage.

He stood quiet, gazing into the flames as he drank every drop of the golden liquor. Finally, he set the glass aside and turned.

Matilda straightened her spine, but maintained the firm grip of her mother's hand.

"How long has this—" He closed his eyes and sighed, holding up the letter again. "Been going on?"

The question seemed direct, but deep inside, the reality was anything but simplistic. Her father demanded an explanation. Her words jumbled in a knot at the base of her throat, choking her.

"Not long." Her inability to defend herself infuriated her. How could she make her father understand her love for Anson? She had to try. "At least not on his part."

Her father cocked his head. "What do you mean?"

"Remember all those years ago, Papa, when you invited the major to my birthday dinner?" She released her mother's hand and stepped closer to her father. "The moment I saw him. I knew there would never be another man in the world for me."

"You were ten, Matilda." He scoffed and set the glass aside.

"Yes, I know. I buried the feelings I harbored for Major Montgomery for years. I tried to find another man, one more suited to my age. Until he broke my heart." She twisted her hands in the fabric of her robe. "Remember how I was after that, Papa? I could not even bear to leave my room."

"I remember." Her mother came beside her. "I begged you to find someone to talk to."

"And I did." She paused. "I wrote to the major. He gave me hope, told me to reach for the man I truly wanted."

"So, you allowed him to steal you from your family, without a word, to another country and shame yourself?" The furrow between his brow deepened.

Matilda shook her head. "The night we met in Paris. He told me that I deserved a better man." She took the letter from her father's trembling hand and held it up. "He said this was a mistake and demanded I forget him to find someone more suitable."

"Oh, sweetheart." Her mother brushed a curl away from Matilda's face.

Tears stung her eyes threatening to spill unchecked. "I could not let him disappear from my life forever. I still loved him. More than ever, if that makes any sense." She chuckled at the absurdity of the situation. "I needed to convince him that I meant every word. That I wanted him and him alone."

"It does not explain the contents of that letter." Her father fumed. "If he wrote those words, then there is truth to them. I will not let the man I trusted for damn near thirty years ruin my only daughter."

"How do you know he has not already ruined me?" Matilda tilted her chin in defiance. "Perhaps he has already ravished me and claimed me as his own."

A deep crimson flush crept up her father's neck, snaking into his face. "Then I will kill him." He turned away and leaned against the bookcase breathing deeply.

Matilda's heart sank. She nestled into her mother's embrace and accepted her comfort.

"Take her away from here." His words lashed her soul. "Go."

She tore from her mother's grasp. "No, do not take me away. Please, I beg you, Papa. I love him. Please." Everything she worked for, all the time she spent convincing Anson that it could work, that they were meant to be together would shatter like a rock colliding with a stained-glass masterpiece. There would be no salvaging it.

"Come now, Matilda." Her mother's soft words and firm hand urged her from the room.

Tears spilled, and she swiped them angrily with the sleeve of her robe. "Let me go, Mama. Let me stay." She pulled her arm, but her mother remained steadfast.

Furious, Matilda relented, hoping to seize the perfect moment to return to Anson. If she could just stop her father from acting on his threat—the wheels in her mind spun.

They retrieved her cloak and shoes before stepping out into the cold. Matilda shivered and followed her mother's lead to the waiting carriage. Inside, she slid to the other side, but the door was sealed. She slumped on the bench and folded her arms. Her mother settled beside her and covered them both with a blanket.

The carriage lurched into motion. Matilda wanted to scream

at the frustration boiling inside of her. Why was her father so averse to their love? Of course, they were friends and it would be a bit awkward in the beginning. But did he not wish for her to be happy? Her frown deepened, and she grumbled beneath her breath.

"Do not fret, Matilda." Her mother rested her hand on hers. "Your father will not kill the major."

"No, but I fear he may do him a great injury none-the-less."

"They have been friends and partners too long to have anything come between them." Her soft smile shone in the passing streetlight. "Even under the duress of extenuating circumstances."

"I am not an extenuating circumstance." She glared at her mother. "I cannot control whom I love any more than I can control the weather."

Her mother sighed. "Your father always showed unwavering support for the major. I believe if it had been handled with a bit more delicacy on your part, as well as Anson's, these theatrics could have been avoided." She waved her hand. "If you wanted to marry him, you should have spoken to your father first."

Matilda stared at her mother. Was she utterly mad? "Father would never have let me marry him then any more than he will now."

"Your father would have tried to protect you, of course, but the major is a stubborn man. The only one who ever seemed able to talk any sense into him was your father. It kept him from imprisonment, even though the agreement led to his permanent exile. Stubborn men, no sense at all."

The words blended together in a confusing jumbled heap in her mind. What was she saying? "The major? Exiled?" This small, innocuous piece of information seemed monumental, but her mother seemed nonplussed by its revelation.

"Yes, dear, did he never tell you?" She shook her head dramatically. "The major spent many years in the army serving the Crown. He was chosen to escort an envoy including the Duke of Netherfield to St. Petersburg by request of the Russian emperor. After their arrival, an incident, caused by a civilian faction rioting against the Russian nobility, caused the death of the duke. The major was charged with negligence and returned to England to stand trial."

Matilda pressed her hand to her open mouth. How had she never known? Of everything they shared, he never told her. Not a word.

"Where are we going?" Matilda leaned hard to the right as the driver made a sharp turn.

"To the hotel, of course. I am sure we will find a solution to all of this unpleasantness in the morning."

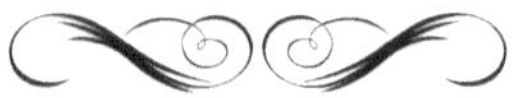

Anson mounted the steps leading to his home in two large strides. *Matilda.*

He paused at the door and frowned when he found it unlocked. He sighed. Of course, he forgot to lock it before he left earlier. He needed sleep. Jacob would arrive as soon as he was able, and that meeting was not one he wished to face in his current state. Sufficient rest and a hearty meal would fortify him enough to face his best friend.

Inside, Anson paused outside his illuminated study. Did *Signora* Castellan return to complete her seduction?

Jacob Hudson stood before the hearth, his face shadowed by the angle of the fire and lamplight. Hope for their reunion shriveled inside him. He inhaled deeply.

"Jacob." He mustered as much geniality as he could. "It is good to see you, my friend." The press of Jacob's lips and his stiff posture concerned him. He held out his hand in offering.

In a burst of movement, Jacob threw a solid punch, hitting Anson across the jaw. A jolt of pain ricochet through his face and up into his head. He stumbled back, his hand cradling his cheek. He eyed his friend warily before straitening to his full height.

"You stole her from us." Jacob's accusation lingered between them.

"I did no such thing." Anson ignored stinging ache pulsing along the right side of his face.

"Then explain this. I found it lying in Matilda's bed chamber the morning we discovered her missing. The very same day you left Paris." He held up the incriminating letter.

Anson groaned and cursed.

"This is your writing. Your signature." Jacob covered the distance between them and thrust the letter into his hands. "Your filthy words penned by your tainted hand in a letter to my daughter." His eyes blazed with fury.

"You have already determined me guilty. Take your pound of flesh if that is what you desire."

"Traitor." Jacob's eyes flashed with a dangerous glint. His hands curled into fists, crushing the letter.

Anson flinched as the sting of that word tore into his soul. Although Jacob referred to the personal betrayal, the wound of his perceived treason bled afresh. The look of anguish on his friend's face twisted guilt around his heart. When he faced the courts, his friend stood beside him, defended him, and offered unwavering support. If not for Jacob, he would have been excommunicated completely. All ties severed. The remaining connection to his home now hung by a tenuous thread.

He considered his words, afraid to push Jacob beyond the brink. "I can offer no excuse for the contents of that letter."

"You admit you led my daughter astray."

Anson shook his head. "I did no such thing. In all the years we conversed, I never crossed the bounds of propriety. Never." He straightened and held Jacob's intense gaze. "In a moment of drunken weakness, I penned that letter pouring the forbidden from my soul. I never intended to mail it." He shrugged. "One of the staff mailed it by mistake."

"You blame your mistake on one of your staff?" Jacob scoffed. "It seems your time abroad has changed you and not for the better."

"It is the truth." Anson's voice rose with the frustration boiling inside him. "What would you have me say?"

"I want the truth."

"I told you the truth." Anson shocked himself with the forcefulness of his reply. "Would you have me bare my soul?" He turned away. "I held her in platonic regard, humoring her curiosity for the world she longed to travel. Matilda's letters gave me a connection to the place I called home. When I longed for England, her words tied me in some inexplicable way to the country I loved. As time passed, it evolved into a friendship I had not foreseen. She trusted me with her heart."

When Anson faced Jacob, his friend stood with his arms folded across his chest. The crumpled letter lay on the floor. Anson retrieved it, smoothing the creases with a gentle hand.

"After her broken engagement, she reached out." He placed the letter on his desk. "My only regret is not telling you from the beginning. You are my oldest and dearest friend, and I should have told you in person when I arrived in Paris earlier this week. I never imagined that Matilda would follow me to Vienna."

"Followed you?"

"Matilda knew I was on that train and purchased a ticket posing as a widow." He smiled at the pure brazenness of such an action on her part. "It was not until the train left the station that I realized she was on board."

"Where did she get the money for the ticket?"

"She saved every allowance you gave her for years in the hope of traveling the continent one day." Anson kicked himself for being so stupid. "She told me as much in her letters. I never anticipated she use it to run away from home."

Jacob shook his head and pressed his fingers to the sides of his temples. "In Paris, when we were at dinner, I saw you speak with her alone. How can I be sure you were not planning your elopement?"

"I can only give you my word."

"Useless." Jacob picked up his coat and put it on. "I have little patience for your lies."

Anson snatched Jacob by the arm. "We have known each other for years. In all those years, I have never lied to you."

"Keeping this a secret was a lie through omission." Jacob pulled his arm away and pushed past Anson.

"Where are you taking her?" He chased him into the hallway.

Jacob stalked toward the door. "I have already taken her somewhere safe. Tomorrow we will return home."

The door slammed closed with a finality that shook Anson's soul. His gaze drifted up the staircase to the empty room Matilda occupied only hours before.

He slammed his fist against the wall, and pain radiated up his arm. He told Jacob the truth of what transpired between Matilda and himself, but it felt hollow and tarnished. A shameful event to hide in darkness. Perhaps he had not been true to himself by denying the simple reality.

He loved her, more than his career, even more than his country. Matilda was gone, beyond his reach forever.

CHAPTER TWENTY-TWO

London, England
December 24, 1899

A month passed and Anson never came. He sent no letter, no explanation, nothing. Why? What happened between her father and Anson? She feared her heart would never again be whole.

They returned to London without incident. She remembered very little of the trip aside from her mother's insistence she attempt to see the bright side of the whole debacle. The train, while lovely, held no appeal after the Alpine Express. The memories of the journey to Vienna brought an aching loneliness that never seemed to ease.

Try as she might, Matilda could not harbor resentment toward her parents. They wished only to protect her. While she appreciated their concern, she knew her own mind well enough to decide whom she wished to spend her life with. She knew since her fateful birthday so long ago.

Matilda hoped to begin a new year with the man she loved. When Anson never arrived, her dream shattered.

Even London looked bleak and shrouded in misery. The buildings and people blurred into the background. As much as she loved London, it no longer felt like home.

Christmas decorations dotted the shops and markets. Her mother encouraged her to find ways to occupy her mind. Together, they trussed the tree with glass ornaments and silver tinsel. They even baked her favorite pastries and invited friends for tea.

These things distracted her, but they did not shake his memory from the forefront of her mind. If anything, her longing intensified.

When she mentioned Anson, her father retreated into his study. He refused to speak his name or acknowledge his existence. She refrained, knowing it would only darken his mood.

Matilda wrote letters every day, posting them herself before her parents woke. But Anson did not reply. Perhaps he was right. She deserved better. If he truly loved her, he would have fought harder.

On Christmas Eve, Elsie appeared outside her door.

"Letter for you, miss." Elsie's eyes glittered with excitement.

Matilda snatched the letter and tore open the seal. Inside, Anson's familiar script made her breath catch.

"Forgive me."

Tears filled her eyes, blurring the words. She sniffed and wiped them away. What did the letter mean? Forgive him for what? For pushing her away. For abandoning her. For breaking her heart. She pinched her eyes closed.

Elsie offered a handkerchief. "Is there anything I can do, miss?"

She dabbed her eyes. Her smile faltered. "No, Elsie. I am afraid not."

"Ring the bell if I can help." Elsie hesitated a moment before retreating.

Matilda closed her bedroom door and stood before the fireplace. The letter in her hand ripped open the tender wound in her heart. She paused for half a breath and dropped the paper into the flames. The parchment curled into smoldering ash, swallowing the words contained within.

Determination replaced the pain. This would not define her. No, her love for the major was not shameful or wrong. She bore her sentiments with pride, even if her family did not understand. The major wished for absolution. So be it. But she would grant it to herself as well.

Matilda squared her shoulders. She spent the last of her tears. No man was worth this much pain. Certainly not Major Anson Montgomery, regardless of how much she still loved him.

With careful attention, Matilda prepared for the Rotham's

annual Christmas Eve ball. She chose her favorite green satin gown with the golden accents and the lovely gold shawl. Her fingers trailed over the special lace made in Italy as she stared at her reflection in the mirror.

The gold and rich forest green accentuated the vivid auburn in her hair. She fastened a single string of pearls around her throat. *Perfect.*

Matilda opened her door and stepped out into the hallway. A deep breath calmed her. Then another. Slowly, the anxiety ebbed away. Determined to enjoy herself, she made her way to the parlor where her parents waited.

"Oh, darling, you look radiant." Her mother beamed at the sight of her.

Her father glanced up from the papers in his hand and nodded. "Lovely." His gaze remained locked on hers.

A sliver of uncertainty wedged into her newly found confidence. Matilda opened her mouth, but instead of speaking, she drew her lower lip between her teeth.

He sighed and set the papers aside before turning to his wife. "My dear, would you please ensure the servants have their direction for the evening?"

"Of course." Matilda's mother squeezed her hand and pressed a kiss to her cheek before leaving the room.

He raked his hand through his hair, the gesture so similar to Anson's it made Matilda's heart ache. She shifted her weight from one foot to the other and pushed him from her mind.

"Is there something you wish to discuss, Papa?" Matilda quelled the flutter in the pit of her stomach.

"Yes." He cleared this throat and drew himself up as if preparing to face something he would rather not. "Do you still love him?"

Matilda blinked, uncertain she heard him correctly. After a month of avoiding all conversation about the major, her father surprised her with his sudden and quite unexpected inquiry.

"Why are you asking me now?" Her frustration bubbled to the surface. "You have made it perfectly clear how you feel about the major."

"As your father, it is my duty to protect you." He spoke in measured tones, but the conflicting emotion in his voice resonated like gunfire. "Put yourself in my position for a moment." His hands balled into fists, clenching and unclenching several times before he continued. "What was I to think when you vanished and the only clue to your whereabouts pointed toward the one man I thought I could trust?"

Shame flooded her face with heat. Matilda refused to succumb to its demand. "If I would have told you, if I would have come before you and asked your permission, would you have granted it?"

His jaw clenched, but he did not respond.

"I have apologized a dozen times." She shook her head and scoffed. "But you refuse to listen. Anson did not pursue me. Even now, he has cut me from his life. I mean nothing to him. Less than nothing." Tears blurred her vision. "If he loved me, he would have come. He would have fought for me."

"Matilda." Her father's soft voice enveloped her before his embrace. She leaned into his strength and allowed his warmth to soothe the pain. "I am sorry, my dear. For everything. It is never a father's wish to see his child suffer."

Her sobs slowed, but her father held her tight. "Papa, I have been a fool."

"We both have." He tipped her chin up and wiped the tears from her cheeks with his handkerchief. "Shall we begin anew?"

Matilda nodded. The determination she felt earlier in her bed chamber returned with renewed purpose. The pain of rejection still stung, but her parents offered both understanding and comfort. She would find joy again, even if it meant a life without the major.

"The carriage is here, my love." Her mother stood in the doorway, her eyes misty, hands clasped against her breast. "Come, let us enjoy our Christmas celebration."

After taking a few moments to freshen up, Matilda joined her parents in the waiting carriage. Within twenty minutes, they arrived at the Rotham's estate on the edge of London. Though there were few of noble standing in attendance, although most of the guests moved in prestigious circles throughout the country. Businessmen, politicians, educators, and so forth mingled in mixed company at this highly anticipated event.

Matilda often found the socialization tedious. However, she loved dancing, almost as much as she loved reading, and this ball always indulged her heart's desire.

She gathered with a few of her friends near the balcony doors. The ladies chatted and compared dance cards, but Matilda's enthusiasm dissipated with every passing moment. Of all the men in the room, she found none who captured her interest.

"So much for dancing," she muttered under her breath and sighed. Her gaze swept the room. Thick ropes of green and red garland strung between each pillar. Gold and silver tinsel hung like ice sickles from the pine wreaths. Red velvet bows punctuated each door.

The soft strains of a waltz filled the room. Longing filled her heart, threatening to crack it in two. Her body swayed to the music. Her feet rose and fell, ready to carry her to the dance floor. She dropped her gaze and squeezed the dance card in her fist.

"May I have this dance?"

The music drifted into the distance. Her heart ceased beating. Matilda turned. "Anson."

He looked handsome and distinguished in a dashing black suit with a splash of emerald green across his waist, a red handkerchief in his pocket, and a white tie around his throat. The silver at his temples blended perfectly into his dark hair. When he smiled, those dimples flashed and all coherent thought fled.

"What…" Her question melted on her tongue when he took her hand and led her onto the dance floor. Her companions stared, their mouths gaping. She ignored them and focused on the man holding her hand.

Pure bliss settled over her. He placed one hand on her hip and grasped her hand in the other. When he drew her into the steps, her bodice brushed against his broad chest. His heat mingled with his intoxicating scent and a thousand memories flooded her. The letters. The train. His kiss. His promise.

The world faded around them as they danced. Matilda met his gaze, drowning in the fathomless glacier blue depths.

"I must be dreaming."

He shook his head and smiled. The dimples appeared once more.

She remembered his letter. *Forgive me.* Her gaze narrowed. "Why are you here?"

"I missed you."

"If my father sees you…"

"He invited me."

"What do you mean?" She shook her head certain she misheard him.

"When you left Vienna, I realized what a fool I had been. I spent the last few weeks preparing for this moment, with your father's blessing, of course." His gaze rekindled the hope she abandoned at his silence. "I love you, Matilda, and I cannot bear another moment without you."

"You do?" Matilda tripped over her feet as they spun. Speechless, she clung to him.

"Yes, more than anything." Anson guided her effortlessly through the dancing couples as the music drew to a close.

When he released her, she shivered at the loss of contact. When he took her hand and led her from the crowd, she followed willingly. For the past month, she longed for this man. Even a simple letter would have sufficed. Never did she imagined he would appear and profess his love to her as if in a dream.

They wove through the crowd. Some of the gentlemen watched with interest, their gaze lingering as they passed. Several ladies whispered behind their fans. Their narrowed gazes made Matilda uncomfortable.

"Where are you taking me?" She stumbled behind him.

They stepped into a parlor down the hall from the ballroom. Matilda gasped. A ten-foot Christmas tree gilded in rich vibrant garland and bedecked with sparkling glass ornaments winked from the corner of the room. Opposite lay a hearth boasting a warm and welcoming blaze. Matilda spun in a circle, appreciating the festive space.

Anson leaned against the door, tucking the key in his waistcoat pocket. His gaze darkened. Hunger burned in their depths, sharper and more prominent than she ever saw during their time together.

She pressed her hands to her cheeks. Heat overwhelmed her. If he were a predator and she the prey, she would have sacrificed herself just to be consumed by the ecstasy he offered. As if he read her thoughts, he stepped closer.

"I missed you, Matilda."

She turned away, unable to contain the riot of emotion thundering through her. For so long she prayed he would come for her. Reality tasted bittersweet.

Nothing prepared her for the surge of emotion that enveloped her as he wrapped his arms around her, pulling her tightly into his warmth. One hand splayed across her stomach while the other cupped her jaw. His fingertips played along the sensitive skin of her throat. She leaned against him and closed her eyes relishing the protective embrace. He spun her slowly to face him.

"I should never have pushed you away." His hands flexed against her back. "I still stand by my assertion; you deserve a better man."

"I do not want any other man." She cradled his face between her hands. "I only want you."

"You do not know what kind of man I am."

"You are a good man."

He shook his head. "They called me a traitor. Can you love a man banished from the country he served faithfully for sixteen years?" The words fell from his lips in a rush, as though vocalizing the words tainted him.

"I do not understand. I know about the envoy to St. Petersburg and the incident that ended your military career." She bit her lip, unsure of how to show him this information did not tarnish him in her eyes. "Why would this affect how I feel about you?"

"It may not affect how you feel about me, but it certainly affects our relationship." He sat in the wingback chair near the fire. Her heart ached at the loss of contact until he pulled her into his lap. Face to face, he met her gaze with unblinking certainty. "I should have told you this long ago."

"Tell me now."

"Your father defended me throughout the trial. Even with the best legal counsel, I was dishonorably discharged from the military and exiled from England by request of the duke's family." His brow furrowed. "It was only because of your father I was able to continue working for the British government. Jacob persuaded some members of parliament that I could still serve my country. The caveat being I could never return to England. I could only report by currier."

"That is why you never returned." The unwavering conviction of Anson's actions, his history, and his respect for her father came together in an explosion of understanding. She jumped from his lap. "Why are you here then? What if they discover you are here? They will arrest you!"

Anson rose to his feet and shook his head. "I do not plan on staying. Besides, it has been eleven years since they sentenced me. I doubt they would even flinch if they knew I were here."

She relaxed at his words. "But you sacrificed everything for your country."

He shrugged. "Nothing mattered more than my duty to the Crown and the safety of her people." His fierce gaze stole her breath. He ran a finger along her cheek. "Until you."

The heat of his touch melted her insides. "Why did you never marry?"

"I never found a person worthy of my devotion, my protection, my love." His gaze dropped to her lips before he spoke again. "I may have betrayed my country and my best friend, but I will be damned if I betray my heart."

Anson kissed her. Soft, silken heat unraveled inside her. She wrapped her arms around his neck, pulling him closer, wanting more. He deepened the kiss, breaching her lips, seeking her tongue with his own. The taste of desperation and the smoky hint of whisky mingled with Anson's warm spicy scent. The welcoming aroma of home and hearth drew her deeper into his embrace.

She was home. Anson was her home.

Alpine Express
January 1, 1900

The corridor lay deserted. Anson quickened his pace in anticipation. He spent a small fortune securing the suite compartment on the Alpine Express. As this was his first night as a married man, he conceded a small indulgence. His wife deserved every comfort while they traveled home to Vienna. They both did.

After a small, intimate ceremony at her parent's home, the couple caught the first boat to Paris where they boarded the Alpine Express. Once they boarded the train where the madness began nearly two months earlier, Anson relaxed. After dinner in the dining car, he made arrangements for breakfast in their compartment while Matilda retired for the evening.

His pulse quickened at the thought of his wife in their bed. Since that first kiss, he longed for more. Restraint had never been hard for Anson. At least until Matilda.

After a month of negotiation and begging, Jacob finally conceded. A Christmas miracle. The truth was evident, Anson loved Matilda and would do whatever was necessary to marry her.

With Jacob and Diana's blessing, they were united. Nothing could keep him from Matilda. Not his conscience, not his friendship, not his duty to queen and county. She was his wife.

Anson unlocked the compartment door and stepped into the luxurious room. A table and two chairs sat in front of the window. The water closet lay beyond a closed door to his left. On the right, an oversized bed lay empty. He frowned.

He closed the door behind him and locked it. The sound of

running water echoed from the water closet. With a grin, he opened it and leaned against the frame. His gaze drifted over the white silk clinging to his wife's curves as she leaned over the sink.

He drew her against him with one arm. His cock pressed against her soft backside.

"Anson." She straightened, and he adjusted his grip, locking her firmly in his embrace. Their gaze met in the mirror.

He pressed a kiss to her neck. She moaned and arched deeper into him. All restraint vanished.

She spun in his embrace, and he let her shift before tightening his grip once more.

"Good evening, husband." Her purr sent a wave of lust cascading through him.

"Wife." He kissed her and lost all sense.

He pulled her to the bed and sat, dragging her across his lap. As he explored her mouth, his left hand cradled her against him while the right slid along her leg. It inched up the fabric until his fingers brushed the inside of her bare thighs.

Matilda gasped and wiggled against him.

He smiled against her mouth. "Open for me, sweetheart." He nudged her thighs apart with his fingertips. Cool air soothed the aching heat at her center. Her fingers gripped the fabric of his shirt when his warm touch found her most intimate place.

"Oh, my heavens." She panted as he caressed her.

"Look at me." He basked in her reaction to his touch. Every stroke brought a soft moan from her lips.

He ignored his body's demands and focused only on her needs. She struggled to hold his gaze as the intimacy of the moment overwhelmed her.

"Breathe, my love."

Matilda inhaled deeply. He slipped two of his fingers deep inside her slick channel. Her grip tightened as he moved his fingers, in and out. Anson moved slow, until she relaxed against him and moaned. He quickened his pace.

She lay across his lap, her legs parted like a wanton harlot on display. Anson explored her, kissed her with a passion she could never have imagined. His thumb brushed against the apex of her sex, and she writhed against him. He circled the swollen nub with his thumb as he thrust his fingers into her heat. She arched her hips against him.

"Beautiful." Anson kissed the corner of her mouth. He quickened his pace.

Matilda stiffened against him, her body trembling. Anson's name tumbled from her lips in a mumbled litany.

Anson never saw a more beautiful sight. Matilda opened her eyes, cheeks flushed pink, her body sated. He smiled, admiring his wife in the afterglow of her orgasm. She buried her face in his chest.

"No time for modesty, wife." He pressed a kiss to her forehead. "I love watching you come apart in my arms. At my mercy."

"I fully intend to finish what I started on this train in November." Matilda climbed from the bed. Her satin gown draped precariously low across her bosom.

Oh, sweet mercy. The gown accentuated every delicious swell and curve. Her red curls hung over her shoulder and brushed the heavy swell of her pink-tipped breasts. He longed to take those nipples between his teeth until she screamed with pleasure. The sweet juncture of her thighs crowned with auburn curls tormented him. His cock twitched imagining those long legs wrapped around him when he found his own release.

She drew her lip between her teeth, and he groaned. Anson stood and unbuttoned his shirt, carefully observing the gentle rise and fall of her breasts quickening with every button he released from its tiny moor. When he pulled the fabric from his shoulders, she swore.

Anson smiled. "Touch me, love."

A blush stole along her chest and into her cheeks. She reached for his trousers. Her gaze dropped to his hands.

"Let me."

Anson dropped his hands to his side. Matilda's eager fingers brushed against his stomach as she grasped the trousers. She made quick work of the buttons and hooked her thumbs into the fabric before pushing it down. He tossed the fabric aside. When he stood, there was no mistaking the gleam of curiosity in her gaze at the sight of his cock.

"You wanted to touch me."

Matilda met his gaze and pressed her left hand to his chest. Her fingers tangled in the hair, the questing touch arousing him more. Her right hand wrapped around his cock, and all the air in his lungs whooshed out. He gasped for breath at her steady, confident grip.

It had been years since a woman touched him, especially with such bold determination. He wrapped his hand around hers and eased her off.

"The night will be over quickly if you persist, my love." He knew a few strokes, and she would have him spending like a randy school boy.

"You told me I could touch you." She pouted.

"We have the rest of our lives." He pulled her into his arms and kissed her soft lips. Lord, he could not wait until she wrapped them around his cock. Later. This night was about her, and her alone. He could seduce her every night for the rest of his life, and it would never be enough. This woman consumed him entirely.

With her, he felt complete. Home.

Her sweet taste melted on his tongue like the finest chocolate. He lifted her in his arms and laid her down beneath him on the thick coverlet. When he nestled himself between her thighs, his cock brushed against her entrance.

"Yes, Anson. Please."

With those words, Anson lost all rational control. He pushed inside her heat and cursed his lack of restraint. She arched and moaned. He peppered her lips and cheek with soft kisses in an effort to soothe her. His body demanded to claim her completely. He fought the urge to thrust deep into her warmth.

When her encouraging cries reached his ears, he quickened his pace. The world around him dimmed. In this moment, it was only him and Matilda entwined together.

"More, please, more."

Anson obliged, thrusting with measured strokes, angling his hips to stroke the sensitive spot nestled in her curls. Her cries echoed in the room, urging him onward, higher and higher, until she shattered and trembled in his arms. The sweet clench of her walls around his cock pushed him over the edge, and he tumbled headfirst into the blissful oblivion of pleasure.

Dazed, he leaned his forehead against her shoulder, careful not to lean his full weight into her. The soft press of her lips against his skin brought him back to the present. He leaned back and searched her face.

A sheen of perspiration gave her a damn near ethereal glow. He brushed a curl from her forehead. She grinned.

"That was wonderful."

Anson returned her grin and placed a lingering kiss on her lips. "Yes, it was, my love." He rose from the bed. "Wait here."

He retreated to the water closet. After cleaning himself quickly, he returned with a wet cloth for Matilda. He cleaned her, watching her silly expressions as he tended to her needs. She tried to do it herself, but Anson insisted.

"It is my duty to care for my wife." He laid the rag aside.

Anson leaned against the headboard and pulled her into his arms. They lay quietly basking in the afterglow of their lovemaking.

"That was wonderful." Matilda nestled against him, her arm draped across his chest, her thigh across his.

He stroked his fingertips across her bare shoulder.

"Anson." Her breath tickled his skin. "What took you so long?"

"What do you mean?"

"When I left Vienna, it took until Christmas for you to come for me, even though you admit you realized what a fool you had been the moment Papa told you I was gone."

"Jacob would never let you go unless I could prove myself." He pressed a kiss to her forehead. "I know him well. I am quite surprised it did not end in bloodshed, quite honestly."

She laughed. The sound warmed his heart. "I guess it is strange for a man to fall in love with his best friend's daughter."

"Quite." Anson agreed.

She shifted and climbed astride him. "I am very pleased you came around. It took you long enough."

His arousal stirred once more. "Seems I must make up for lost time then."

"I am at your mercy, major."

He sank into her. "I love you, Matilda."

"I love you too."

EPILOGUE

Vienna, Austria
Late January 1900

"Darling." Matilda called from the hallway. "You have a parcel."

At the sound of his wife's voice, Anson set aside the letter he just opened. He had been ignoring the mail on his desk. Three letters in and the sound of his wife's voice already drove him to distraction.

"Bring it in the study, my love."

"Oh, do I have permission to enter now?" She stood in the doorway with the parcel in her hand.

"I need to get some work accomplished, Matilda." He beckoned her closer with a crook of his finger. She approached with an exaggerated sway of her hips and placed the parcel on his desk before sitting on his lap. "I find your presence distracting."

"My apologies, darling. But this seemed important." She gestured to the brown wrapped parcel with an unfamiliar postmark.

He kissed her and shooed her from his lap.

She watched in fascination as he cut through the wrapping. "What could it be?"

He unfurled the brown paper and stared at the contents. His journal. He blinked in surprise, flipped through the pages. Yes, it was his handwriting. Unease and concern wove through him.

"Who delivered this?"

Matilda shook her head, her eyes wide. "A delivery boy. There was no return address. What is it?"

"My journal." He shook his head. "I misplaced it on the Alpine Express last November."

"How strange." Matilda ran her fingers across the leather cover. "Gertrude also misplaced her journal during that trip."

Anson glanced up. "Wait, she had a leather journal go missing as well?"

"Well, yes, but she found hers before—"

"Did you see the journal?" Anson gripped wife's hand.

Matilda nodded. "I caught a glimpse of it." She looked at Anson's journal again and paused. "Well, that is strange."

"What is?"

"Gertrude's journal bore these exact initials." Her gaze locked on his. "I saw the same initials on the journal I found in your desk the night we arrived in Vienna." She pressed her hand to her mouth. "You cannot possibly think—"

"That your sweet, unassuming friend Gertrude is a thief. Yes, I most certainly do think that." Anson thumbed through the journal searching for one specific page. Jagged edges lay where the pages had been torn. "That Russian bastard is in on it too."

"Mr. Voronia? Why would they take your journal?"

"Because I kept meticulous notes on everyone I interacted with in that journal." His gaze hardened at the thought of Nikolai using him so blatantly. "It listed my sources concerning Nikolai's ties to the Okhrana."

"What is the Okhrana?"

"Russian secret police."

"I do not understand." She took Anson's hands. "Why would he betray you? You are friends."

"A tenuous description at best." He frowned. "Nikolai and I share a much more complicated history than anyone knows."

"Tell me."

Anson shook his head. "Not until I find him. Suffice it to say, I owe my life to Nikolai, and that bastard knows it."

"What are you going to do?"

"I am going to hunt down the traitor and demand an explanation before I kill him. He owes me that much."

"Do not rush to judgement." Matilda soothed him. "Perhaps the journal was a misunderstanding. Why else would he return it?"

"He has taken what he needs." Anson sighed. "Now I must sort through it and see what else he took."

Matilda stood on her tip toes and pressed a kiss to his lips. He held her tight, deepening the kiss for a brief second before releasing her.

"Go, before I ravish you and forget all about this."

"Promises, promises." She tossed a wink over her shoulder as she walked out the door.

Anson collapsed in his chair. What the hell was he going to do with Nikolai? Both he and Fräulein Bleul vanished completely. He raked his hand through his hair and sighed. That was the problem with Nikolai, always secrets and lies.

It was about time someone uncovered them.

The End

For Nikolai and Gertrude's story read
Temptation on the Alpine Express

OTHER BOOKS BY KIRSTEN S. BLACKETER

<u>CRAVING 1985 SERIES</u>
When I Found You
Can't Fight This Feeling
She Gives Love a Bad Name
Owner of a Lonely Heart
Just What I Needed

<u>HISTORICAL</u>
An Irresistible Shadow
A Shadow's Kiss
Mississippi Moonshine
Deceiving the Earl
Jewel of Winter
At Winter's Demand
Under Winter's Control
Seducing Winter's Gentleman
Stealing the Widow's Heart
Seduction on the Alpine Express
Temptation on the Alpine Express

<u>CONTEMPORARY</u>
A Lockdown Love Affair
A Holiday Love Affair
Mistletoe and Mistakes
Confessions of a Fangirl
Confessions of a Gamer Girl
Confessions of a Glamour Girl
The Flight Before Christmas

<u>FANTASY/FAIRYTALE</u>
Curse of the Huntsman's Jewel
The Huntsman's Revenge

<u>PIRATES AND PERSUASION</u>
Queen Takes Hook

ABOUT THE AUTHOR
KIRSTEN S. BLACKETER

Kirsten S. Blacketer is a multi-published indie author of both historical and contemporary romance. When she's not writing, she homeschools her two children and enjoys time with her family. In those moments of freedom, she devours romance novels while sipping a glass of wine. Age has only shown her that writing villains can be just as fun as heroes. Her next life goals are to write a New York Times Bestseller and one day have Adam Driver play a starring role in a film version of one of her books. A girl can dream, right?

Read more at **http://kirstensblacketer.com.**

ALSO WRITES AS JEN BRADLEE